Mrs. J. H. Riddell

Mortomley's estate

A Novel. Vol. 3

Mrs. J. H. Riddell

Mortomley's estate
A Novel. Vol. 3

ISBN/EAN: 9783337046460

Printed in Europe, USA, Canada, Australia, Japan

Cover: Foto ©Andreas Hilbeck / pixelio.de

More available books at **www.hansebooks.com**

MORTOMLEY'S ESTATE.

A Novel.

BY

MRS. RIDDELL,

AUTHOR OF

'GEORGE GEITH," "TOO MUCH ALONE," "HOME, SWEET HOME,"
"THE EARL'S PROMISE," ETC. ETC.

IN THREE VOLUMES.

VOL. III.

LONDON:

TINSLEY BROTHERS, 8 CATHERINE STREET STRAND

1874.

PRINTED BY TAYLOR AND CO.,
LITTLE QUEEN STREET, LINCOLN'S INN FIELDS.

CONTENTS.

— ◆ —

MORTOMLEY'S ESTATE.

CHAPTER I.

THE MEETING OF CREDITORS.

IF any person ever questioned the wisdom of Mr. Asherill in taking for his partner that perfect gentleman Mr. Swanland, his doubts must have been dispelled had he chanced to be present at the meeting of creditors—*re* Archibald Mortomley.

Mr. Asherill himself would have felt proud of his junior, had his principles permitted of his attending on the occasion.

There was a judicial calmness about Mr. Swanland, which produced its effect on even the most refractory member of that motley throng.

It would have been almost as easy for a creditor to question the decision of a Vice-Chancellor, as the statements of that unprejudiced accountant.

If Mr. Swanland did not fling back his coat and unbutton his waistcoat, and tear open his shirt and request those present to look into his heart, and see if falsehood could there find a resting-place, he, at least, posed himself as Justice, and held the scales, I am bound to state, with strict impartiality between debtor and creditor.

His worst enemy could not say he favoured either. If his own brother had gone into liquidation, he would not have turned the beam against the creditors in favour of that misguided man.

Even-handed justice was meted out in Salisbury House. The old fable of the two animals that stole the cheese, and asked a wiser than themselves to decide as to the share to which each was entitled, was put on the boards there, and acted day after day, and with a like result. In their earnest desire to be perfectly impartial towards both sides, Messrs. Asherill and Swanland ate up the cheese themselves.

If this proceeding failed to satisfy either creditor or debtor, it was no fault of theirs.

No one could say they had shown favouritism; and, indeed, it would have been very wicked if any one had, since Mr. Asherill—and inclusively Mr. Swanland—always declared each estate as it came, and was liquidated, left them losers by the transaction. Nevertheless, the villa residences of both gentlemen bore no evidence of poverty; on the contrary—though had either partner taken the trouble to visit the houses of those who were so ill-advised as to go into liquidation instead of bankruptcy, he would have found that the " friendly arrangement" carried on under the paternal eye of Mr. Asherill, or the dispassionate gaze of Mr. Swanland, had not resulted in any increase of luxury for the debtors or their families.

Like his senior, however, Mr. Swanland was utterly indifferent to the ruin of his clients, so long as he compassed his own success.

Heaven forbid I should say that all men of his profession are cast in the same mould, but there can be no question that the new law throws a fearful amount of power into the hands of any one who likes to use it for his own advantage, and places at the same time any trustee who desires to deal leniently with a bankrupt in a position of unpleasant responsibility.

To put the matter plainly, if a trustee has a fancy for the cheese, he can eat it himself, rind and all; but if he thinks this creditor has been hardly done by, or that the debtor is a poor devil, really very much to be pitied, he had better take care how he gives expression to such sentiments.

It is far wiser to adopt Mr. Swanland's *rôle*, and please nobody, than run the risk of trying to please anybody but himself.

But at a meeting of creditors when his mission was to tell a flattering tale and get the ear of the assemblage, Mr. Swanland was a man of whom his partner felt justly proud.

What could be neater than the way in

which he placed the state of affairs, *so far as his information went,* before the bulls of Bashan with whom he had to deal.

Like oil on the waters came the flow of Mr. Swanland's fluent tongue.

He uttered no disparagement of Mortomley. His position was unfortunate, doubtless, and so was the position of his creditors, but Mr. Swanland was pleased to inform the meeting that he expected the estate to return a very good dividend; a very good dividend indeed.

From what he could hear and from what he had seen, he was justified in saying a large profit could be realized by carrying on the works. There were a fine plant, an extensive connection, and a considerable amount of stock.

It was perhaps unfortunate that Mr. Mortomley had not sooner taken his creditors into his confidence; but, said Mr. Swanland with a touching humility that might have done credit to Mr. Asherill himself, "we are all liable to error."

"Mr. Mortomley acted for the best, no doubt." Here there was a murmur of dissent from the bulk of the audience, "but whether it has proved for the best or not in the past, at all events he has acted wisely in the present by relinquishing everything to his creditors."

Here one sceptical wretch suggested "he hadn't given anything up till he couldn't help hisself."

Which was indeed a statement too perfectly true to be controverted.

Mr. Swanland therefore glossed it over. "No doubt," he said, "Mr. Mortomley would have done better for himself, and—others— had he consulted his friends and creditors at an earlier stage of his embarrassments, but even as matters stood, it afforded him, Mr. Swanland, much gratification to be able to state that no real cause existed for the gloomy view of affairs taken by a few of the gentlemen in the room.

"He begged to be allowed to lay before the meeting a statement of Mr. Mortomley's liabilities and probable assets." Which he did.

It was no part of Mr. Swanland's policy

at this period to cover his canvas with dark colours.

Rather he went in for Turneresque effects, and threw a lurid light upon the profits which might be expected from the continuance of the business under *proper supervision*; from the leasing of Homewood and its grounds to a suitable and responsible tenant; from the sale of the effects; from the collection of the outstanding book debts, and the appropriation of the remaining portion of Mrs. Mortomley's fortune.

When he came to this last part of his story, over which he was rather inclined to slur, as an inexperienced pianist slurs a difficult passage in a new piece of music, the knowing ones amongst the creditors pricked up their ears, and one of them, a gentleman who was quite as sharp in his way as Mr. Gibbons, and a vast deal more honest, said,

"If you tell us, Mr. Swanland, how much the estate can pay in cash now, we had better take that amount than await the result of liquidation; whether it be a shilling, half-a-crown, or five shillings in the pound, I say let us all agree to take whatever the estate can pay, and give the bankrupt his discharge. Then if he is honest he can begin again and pay us all off; and if he is not honest, we shall not be one bit worse off than if we allow the concern to go on and stand by watching the whole estate eaten up by lawyers and accountants."

There was a horrible pause; a pause during which Mr. Forde turned sick with terror and Mr. Swanland white with rage, and more than one non-fluent creditor cleared his throat and wetted his lips preparatory to following the suit of the last speaker, and expressing his own humble opinion about the subject on hand.

That pause was broken by Kleinwort.

"I mean not to be rude," he began in his broken English, which was no better and no worse than on that evil day (for England) when he first landed at Folkestone, " but might I make bold to inquire how large is the little stake of that last speaker so confident, in the estate of our poor sick Mortomley?"

"Our little stake, Mr. Kleinwort," answered

the opposing creditor, "is not quite three hundred pounds; but still three hundred pounds is more than I and my partner care to lose totally if we can get anything out of the fire. To the majority of people, this liquidation business is as a new toy. Creditors are delighted with it at first. We have had some experience of its working, however; and when a man goes into bankruptcy we write his account down "doubtful," when he goes into liquidation we write it off "bad."

Then arose a babel of tongues. Mr. Forde, Mr. Kleinwort, Mr. Gibbons, and a host of other creditors, talking all at once, none listening.

To all intents and purposes there was not the slightest necessity for this expression of opinions. Mortomley's affairs had been all settled before the meeting of his creditors was convened. Forde had spoken, and Kleinwort had spoken, and a few other people besides, who amongst them virtually arranged the programme of his business future; and though an Act of Parliament rendered this crush, by intimation, indispensable as a matter of formality, it was, in reality, perfectly useless as a matter of fact.

The only possible pleasure or advantage the most persistent of the smaller creditors could derive from attending the meeting, was the opportunity it afforded him of bemoaning his own hard fortune, and the wickedness of Mortomley in having omitted to settle his little account at all events.

It did not signify in the least that to these lamentations no one listened, unless, indeed, some man gifted with a louder voice and greater powers of endurance than his neighbours compelled the attention of the trustee, who was always able to silence him with some calm and plausible answer,—the indignant creditor had spoken aloud and " given them a piece of his mind straight out,"—while, so far as Mr. Swanland was concerned, his experience had taught him that these ebullitions were all so many safety valves which prevented the possibility of any serious explosion damaging his interests.

At last it became patent even to the representative man who always announces his intention of "attending the meeting personally," of "seeing to his own matters for hisself," and who generally tells the assembled company that all he wants is his money—and his money he will have—that the large creditors were with the trustee; and as the trustee, they considered, must be friendly to Mortomley, there was no use in pushing opposition further.

And indeed there was not. A certain number of creditors who did not "wish to do Mr. Mortomley any harm," who had found Mr. Mortomley a very fair dealing gentleman, and hoped he would get through his trouble all right," had readily agreed to everything Mr. Benning's managing clerk proposed in Mr. Mortomley's interest, and the result was that the amount required and the numbers required to carry a majority had all been made up long before the meeting.

Nevertheless, as he blandly suggested, Mr. Swanland liked to see unanimity amongst the creditors. Kleinwort backing him up with a remark to the effect that "the goods of one was for the goods of all."

"If I get my money," he observed to one splenetic individual, "you get your money. If I get not mine, you get not yours; but look how big is mine besides your little dot; and I am content to wait and believe. Be you content too."

Over the choice of the gentlemen who were to form the committee of management, and who were popularly supposed to be placed on a higher pinnacle of power than that occupied by Mr. Swanland, there proved, however, more difficulty than the trustee bargained for.

Not that it mattered materially to him; but opposition in any shape chafed a temper by no means angelic, induced to a certain degree, perhaps, by a digestion far from good.

And whatever was proposed, Mr. Gibbons and the gentleman who entertained that rabid antipathy against lawyers and accountants set themselves determinedly to oppose; the last individual illustrating his remarks with a candour which, if some people in the City did not fear the strong lights of a court as much as ladies of a certain age dread the unflattering glare of sunshine, would infallibly have produced more than one action for libel.

The only real fun which could be taken out of the meeting arose from this person's comments on the capabilities for evil and impotency for good possessed by the various candidates mentioned, and the assemblage was almost restored to good humour when his plain speaking culminated in a direct attack on Mr. Gibbons concerning the very estate on the management of which that gentleman had prided himself so much when addressing Rupert Halling.

"If I had known Mortomley contemplated any step of this kind," he finished, "I would have taken out a debtor's summons and forced him into the Bankruptcy Court, which he may still live to wish I had done. I hate hole-and-corner work, and all this management of a man's assets and debts in any shabby office on a two-pair back, with some fellow out of a loan-office, or who has been clerk to some disreputable attorney for trustee."

"I apprehend, sir," Mr. Forde was beginning, when Mr. Kleinwort interposed.

"It is of no good use, Forde, talking to this gentleman gifted with so much language. He thinks he is on the floor of your House of Commons, or making his last address to his British public from an Old Bailey dock."

"Bravo! Kleinwort," said Mr. Benning, as a peal of laughter rewarded this utterance.

"German thief," observed his adversary, quite audibly. Then addressing the assemblage, added, "If you are all such idiots as to believe in any statement of accounts dished up at a meeting of creditors such as this; if you refuse to back me up, and are afraid to fight for the recovery of your own money, it is of no use my speaking any longer. I wish you joy, gentlemen, of the dividend you will receive out of this estate."

And with a mocking bow he left the room followed by Rupert Halling, who, slipping his arm through his, walked with him along Cannon Street, saying,

"I wish—I wish we could undo all that has been done in this matter; that my uncle's estate could have been arranged anyhow except in liquidation."

"Well, it cannot now, and there is no use in fretting about the matter," was the reply. "Of course I knew if I talked till Doomsday I could do no good; but I never intend to cease talking till we get some decent sort of Bankruptcy Act. Tell your uncle I bear him no malice, and that I shall be glad to know he has got out of this affair better than I expect. It was not for the sake of the money I spoke, but because I hate to see a good estate eaten up by such fellows as Asherill and Swanland. By the way, that is bad about Mrs. Mortomley's money. How could her husband be such an idiot as not to make her safe!"

"The men who make themselves and families safe are those who let their creditors in," said Rupert sententiously.

" I expect you will find, when Swanland has
finished manipulating the estate, that your
uncle has let his creditors in to a pretty tune,"
answered the other.

" At any rate he has given up everything
he had on earth," remarked Rupert.

" So far as I am concerned, I would much
rather he had kept everything himself than
given it to Swanland.   I should like to meet
that congregation of asses," and he pointed
back towards the Cannon Street Hotel, " two
years hence, and hear what they think of
liquidation by arrangement then."

" I must get back now.   I want to hear the
resolutions," said Rupert.

" Call at my office as you return and let me
know the names of the committee," observed
the other; but Rupert had not the slightest
idea of doing anything of the kind.   He
had promised Dolly to see her husband—who
was at that moment under the same roof with
his creditors, ready to answer any inquiry
they might see fit to put—safe home, and he
meant to fulfil that promise, though home now

meant to his uncle merely that little house at Clapton — though the dear old roof-tree at Whip's Cross might shelter him or his no more for ever.

By the time Rupert re-entered the room, Mr. Swanland had been able to complete the arrangement of Mortomley's affairs to his satisfaction.

The working of the Colour Manufactory was to be continued. A committee of five persons was appointed, and those five persons were Messrs. Forde and Kleinwort ; an opposition colour-maker who, having ordered and paid for some carmine which had not been delivered before the final crash, was thus enabled to take out much more than the value of his money, in helping to undermine the Homewood works, and keep Mortomley himself out of the trade; that friendly creditor who knew nothing of the City, or City ways, and was therefore quite as good as no-one ; and a certain Mr. Lloyd, who said he had no objection to serve on the committee if by doing so he could in any way serve Mr. Mortomley.

In all questions, save one, the majority was to decide any subject in dispute. That one excepted question was the important item of Mr. Mortomley's discharge.

Excepting the five were of one mind on that point, Mr. Mortomley's discharge could never take place. Unless, indeed, he paid ten shillings in the pound — which seeing the power of paying anything had virtually been taken from him, was, to say the least of the matter, an extremely improbable contingency. The gentleman, however, who wished to serve Mr. Mortomley, and Mr. Gibbons, and Mr. Leigh, and a few others, having taken counsel together, a rider was, with much difficulty, appended to the proceedings in the shape of a resolution to the effect that if the committee failed to agree on the subject of the discharge, it should be competent for the bankrupt to refer the matter to another meeting of his creditors, said meeting to be called at his own expense, which, though plausible enough in theory, was a reality no man in Mortomley's position could ever hope, unless a miracle were effected in his favour, to compass.

Moreover, the question of an allowance to Mr. Mortomley was left to the judgment of the committee, and thus everything having been done quite according to law, Mr. Swanland was installed solemnly as trustee and manager of the Mortomley's Estate, and could, the moment he left that room, snap his fingers at all the credulous folks there assembled, Mr. Forde included in that number—Mr. Forde, who expected to sway him as he had swayed other trustees, and who certainly when he elected that Mr. Asherill's perfect gentleman should fill the post of liquidator, never intended his nominee to draw as hard and fast a line against him as against the other creditors.

Very soon, however, he was destined to be undeceived.

He tried to get Mortomley's bills renewed, but Mr. Swanland refused to give him Mortomley's address, and warned him that if he did succeed in obtaining the bankrupt's signature, the documents would not be worth the paper they were written on.

He sent goods to Homewood, but they were returned on his hands.

"I must buy in the best market," said Mr. Swanland. "I am but the agent for the creditors, you will please recollect, and have no power to show favour to any one."

"What the devil do you mean!" inquired Mr. Forde.

"I must buy good articles at the lowest cost price," was the reply; "and your articles are not good, and they are, further, extremely dear?"

"I rather think you forget yourself, sir," said Mr. Forde in his loftiest manner. "You forget I made you trustee of this estate."

"I do not forget; but the days of Queen Victoria are not those of Elizabeth," was the reply. Mr. Swanland, in his hours of elegant leisure, had occasionally met literary people, and though he distrusted them, stored away their utterances and quotations.

"Can't you talk English," asked Mr. Forde in reply.

" Certainly, though I should not care to talk it quite so plainly as did her Majesty. She said, 'I made you, proud prelate, and by —— I will unmake you !' I say, ' You brought this estate to me, and I intend to wind it up honestly without fear or favour.' "

" Damn you ! " said Mr. Forde with a sincerity and vigour the Virgin Queen herself might have envied.

Like Mortomley, whom he had netted, he found himself utterly taken in.

" Would to God ! " he remarked, with that reference to a supreme power people are apt to make when they have exhausted the resources of all their own idols and found them really of very little avail, " Would to God ! I had left the management of Mortomley's Estate to that fool Mortomley himself and his solicitor. They would have considered ME, and this selfish brute will not."

Which was indeed quite true. A man had always better by far place himself in the hands of a man who is a gentleman, even if he be a fool, than of a man who is a cad, even though he be wise.

Save through misadventure, the gentleman will not throw over even a cad; but the cad waits his opportunity and throws over friend and foe, gentle and simple, with equal impartiality.

Mr. Swanland did at all events, and therein, situated as he chanced to be, he was wise.

For with the best intentions in the world, Mr. Forde had hitherto always managed to bring those trustees who were simple enough or dishonest enough to do his bidding to ultimate grief.

When Mr. Swanland spoke of the Manager of the General Chemical Company as so mentally short-sighted that he could only see to twelve o'clock that day, he described his character to a nicety.

Probably, through no fault of his own in the first instance, Mr. Forde eventually found himself traversing a path which led him at one time along the brink of a precipice, at another across a country intersected by deep ravines and dangerous gulleys, and any man who had fully realised the peril of his position must either have abandoned the idea of going further in despair, or have so utterly lost his head as to have been dashed to pieces long before the period when this story opens.

But Mr. Forde did not realise his position, or the position of the General Chemical Company.

He had faith if he could only hold out long enough relief would come—to him—or to the Company. Naturally he hoped it would come to him first, in which case he confided to a few chosen friends the fact that, if he were to walk out of the place, the directors would have to close the wharf-gates within four-and-twenty hours, but if relief were to pay a preliminary visit to the Company, he knew such a stroke of good fortune must ultimately benefit him.

With all his faith, and he had much, he believed Mr. Asherill's partner if appointed trustee of Mortomley's Estate would be with him hand-and-glove, and when he found Mr.

Swanland was not inclined to be hand-and-glove with any man, he bewailed in no measured terms his evil fate to Kleinwort, who only shrugged his shoulders and said,

"You had better much have trusted the sick man and the little lady and the swaggering nephew; you had by far best have had good temper, and not have run to lock them up in liquidation, with your lawyer, your trustee, your committee. That Leigh man might have been turned round a finger—mine—and the little lady and the sick man, had you spoke pleasant, would have gone on trying hard to do their best for another year at least calculation. Those thousands, Forde dear friend, those thousands! Oh! it does break mine heart to call to mind they were so near and are so far! That demon Swanland he will liquidate it all; and we—you Forde and I Kleinwort—we might have dealt with it had I known, had you not spoken so hard to the little woman. I am not much of superstitious, I do hope, dear friend, and yet I feel this will be a bad mistake for us."

Whereupon Mr. Forde bade him hold his tongue if he could not use it to some pleasanter purpose.

But Mr. Kleinwort refused to hold his tongue. "It was not good to lay so many stakes upon that Archibald Mortomley horse," he persisted. "Bah! One that could not, in your charming English, stay, that was a roarer, so short of mercantile breath when you dug your spurs in and flogged him with your heavy whip he dropped down as dead. It was a mistake, and then you made bad worse with the little lady, and for this reason we shall all suffer; we shall all cry and make bitter lamentation."

"Kleinwort, you are enough to drive a fellow mad!" expostulated his so dear Forde.

"Yes, yes, yes. I know all that," said the German. "You never want to hear no speech but what is pleasant and comfortable. You will not listen to warning now, but the bad day may be nearer at hand than you think, when you will say to me, 'You had reason, Kleinwort,'—when you will make remark to others, ' I thought Kleinwort babbled all non-sense, but his words were true words.'"

"Well, whether they prove true or false will not help us in this Mortomley affair now. One good thing is the business being still carried on. That is in our favour."

"You had better make much use of that while you can," was the reply, "for it will not be carried on very long."

"What do you mean?" asked Mr. Forde.

"Just the very thing I say—unlike you English, who always mean not what they say. Swanland will stay colour-maker for while there is money to lose and to spend; but you, even you my good Forde, must know he cannot so conduct that affair as to induce those big works to pay anybody but himself."

"I fail to understand you."

"Could you go down and make those works, of which you know nothing, yield big profits."

"Of course I could," was the confident answer.

"Ah! but you are so clever," said Kleinwort with a sneer, which was lost on his companion. I did forget you had managed so long and so well the Wharf Vedast. It is not many who could bring such talents as you. Swanland has them not most surely, and so I say the Colour Works will stop one day like—that,"—and Mr. Kleinwort clapped his hands together with a suddenness which made his companion jump.

" But he is making an enormous profit," remarked Mr. Forde.

" Ah ! well, we see if we live, if we live not, those who do will see," answered Kleinwort, with philosophical composure, as he parted from his companion.

" I wonder what has come to Kleinwort," thought Mr. Forde ; " until lately he was always hopeful, always pleasant. I hope to mercy nothing is going to happen to him." And at the bare idea, self-suggested, the manager turned pale. " Good Heavens ! what would become of ME in that case ? " was the unspoken sentence which flitted through his mind.

But comfort came to him next instant, in the reflection that let Kleinwort's faults be what they might, they did not include any inclination to deceive his friend.

" He would tell me ; he would give me fair warning ; if there were a leak anywhere, he would not keep the misfortune secret from me," were the assurances with which he restored his own courage.   While all the time the little German was mentally considering,

" That orange is about squeezed dry.   A short time more and our dear Forde will have no more cause to be anxious about the affairs of Kleinwort.   His mind will be set quite at rest.   Bah !   The easement will come sooner than I intended, but it is a wise man can read the signs of the weather.   That new director would spoil our little game if I stopped it not myself.   Yes, it is nearly over, and it is well, though I should like to have played on a little more, and kept Forde like the coffin of Mahomet hanging for a time yet longer."

CHAPTER II.

ONE FRIEND MOST FAITHFUL.

It was Christmas Eve, and Mrs. Mortomley in the little house at Clapton sat "counting out her money."

This ought not to have been a long process, for her resources had sunk very low. Three months had elapsed since her husband's estate went into liquidation, and for those three months, first at Homewood and next at Clapton they had been living on that sum which Rupert's foresight saved from the general wreck, so that the sovereigns lying in Dolly's lap were easily counted. Nevertheless, as though she fancied they might grow more numerous by handling, she let them slip

through her fingers one by one, whilst her eyes
were fastened, not on the glittering gold, but
on the firelight as it now flashed over the small
room and again seemed to die away altogether.

She was quite alone in the house. Susan had
gone out marketing, and Esther, who had long
left Homewood, was visiting her relations in
order to benefit her health, which had suffered
severely during the weeks succeeding to that
dinner-party when Mortomley's friends proved
of so much service to his wife. Rupert, staying
with them, had dragged Mortomley, an unwilling sight-seer up to London, to inspect the
glories of the shops. Lenore was still at
Dassell, and thus it came to pass that Dolly
sat alone in the firelight, counting her money
and thinking prosaically over ways and means.

She had not gone out to meet her trouble half
way, but it was impossible for her to evade the
fact that poverty was coming upon them
like an armed man ; and that although her
husband's health was much improved—miracu-
lously improved said the doctor—it would still
be worse than folly to tell him nothing save a

a few sovereigns stood between them and beggary.

Through all, he had clung to the belief that Dolly's remaining thousands were safe, that she and the child could never know want, and Dolly had lacked courage to open his eyes, and no one else thought it worth while to do so.

As she sat letting the sovereigns fall through her fingers as though they had been beads on a string, Dolly's mind was full of very grave anxiety. She had not taken Rupert into her confidence; a feeling of distrust had arisen in her heart against him, and she did not feel inclined to parade her troubles before a man who, to put the case in its mildest form, was not likely to prove of much assistance to her.

Dolly was at her wits' end—no long journey some of her old detractors would have said—all her early life she and shortness of money had been close acquaintances, but hitherto she and no money had not even shaken hands. A certain income, if small, had always been her or hers within the memory of Dolly; and now, just when she wanted it most, just when even fifty pounds a year would have seemed an anchor upon which to rest, she found herself in London almost without money, with a husband still in a delicate state of health, and without friends.

Yes, indeed, though a score of people at least had written to say how delighted they would be if she and dear Mr. Mortomley would come and pay them a long visit, she felt friendless. To many a kind soul, who knew no better way of sympathizing with their misfortunes than ignoring them, she entertained feelings of the keenest animosity.

Of their conventional little they offered her the best they dared offer. How should they understand that to the Mrs. Mortomley they had known gay and prosperous, her husband's trouble should mean looking after pennies— thinking wearily over sixpences.

In a vague way they understood Mortomley had lost a lot of money, and they at once offered hospitality to his wife and himself; what more could those people do who were totally ignorant of business, and who only

imagined it meant something "horrid in the
City;" but Dolly was smarting just then under
the blows she had received from Messrs. Swanland, Dean, Forde, Kleinwort, Werner, to say
nothing of the other creditors who, in the
Homewood days, had represented to Mortomley's wife that he ought to pay up like a
man, and she failed to do justice to the delicate
if ignorant kindness which tried to make her
comprehend change of circumstances could
produce no coldness with acquaintances who
had shared the festivities of Homewood in the
prosperous days departed.

Dolly was at her wits' end, as I have said.
So far she had honestly been able to pay her
way, but the supplies were running very short
indeed, and she could see no source from which
they could be replenished.

"I might sell my watch," she thought; "I
suppose some jeweller would buy it, but that
money would not last long. I wish I could
teach music or sing or play, or write a novel"
—poor Dolly evidently had the distressed heroine of a work of fiction in her mind—"but I

am a useless little fool; I cannot even do worsted work or embroidery. Archie ought not to have married me; any other woman could think of something; could have done what Lang suggested, for instance," and the head, which still bore its great tower of plaits and frizettes, drooped sadly while she mechanically shifted the remaining sovereigns one after another from hand to hand.

As she sat thus she heard the garden-gate open and shut, but imagining that it had been opened and shut by Susan, she did not alter her position.

Next moment, however, a knock roused her completely, and standing up she went to the door and opened it.

A lady stood on the top step of the flight; but in the darkness, with her eyes blind almost with looking at the firelight and the future, Dolly did not recognize Mrs. Werner.

" Dolly," said the visitor softly.

" Nora," answered Mrs. Mortomley, and then they held one the other in a clinging embrace.

"Come in, dear," Dolly said, and after one look round the house, the poor little house as it seemed to her, unknowing what a haven of refuge it had proved, Mrs. Werner did so.

"I only returned on Friday," Mrs. Werner began, sitting on the sofa and holding both Dolly's hands in hers, "and I could not get over to you on Saturday or yesterday, and I was doubtful about to-day, and consequently did not write, but I wanted to see you so much, your letters have been so short and unsatisfactory. You must tell me everything. First, how is your husband?"

"Better," answered Mrs. Mortomley. "Better, but not well. He has gone to London with Rupert to see the Christmas show set out in the shop windows," Dolly added with a curious smile.

"What is he doing?" asked her friend.

"What can he do? what will they let him do?" Dolly retorted. "He might get a situation at a pound a week, perhaps, if he were strong and well. Don't, Leonora, you hurt me."

"I beg your pardon, darling," said Mrs. Werner, releasing her grasp of Dolly's hands, and kissing one after another of the fingers she had unconsciously clasped so tight; "I did not mean to hurt you, but you ought not to speak in that way, you should not say such things."

"I speak the truth," answered Mrs. Mortomley. "It is not likely you should be able to realise our position. I could not have imagined that any man living in England could, unless he were in prison, be so utterly powerless to help himself as Archie is now. When I said he might earn a pound a week if well and strong, I was in error. He could do nothing of the kind. He is bound to obey Mr. Swanland's bidding. He is his servant. While he was too ill to leave the house, Mr. Swanland graciously excused his attendance at Salisbury House; but now that he is better he has to go there for hours each day, whether it is wet or dry, hail, rain, or sunshine."

"But he is paid for going, of course," suggested Mrs. Werner.

"He certainly has not been paid yet,"

retorted Dolly; "and, what is more, Mr. Swanland is not bound to pay him a penny."

"Then I am sure I should not go were I in his place."

"He is obliged to go," answered Mrs. Mortomley. "There is no use mincing the matter. Archie is as utterly a slave as if his creditors had bought him body and soul. I do not know how he bears it; why he is able to bear it; or rather I do. If he understood our actual position, he would go mad."

"Have you not told him, then?" asked Mrs. Werner in amazement.

"No, I dare not tell him."

"You ought to do so—"

"I ought not, Leonora. Time enough to let him know we are utterly beggared when he is strong to bear the shock. Some day, of course, he must be told, but I shall defer the evil time as long as possible."

Mrs. Werner sighed. She looked round the small rooms and then at Dolly's changed face before she spoke again.

"And so everything was sold at Homewood?" she remarked at last.

"Everything," was the reply. "In the house, that is to say. The works are still carried on. Mr. Swanland wrote to Archie to say we could have the furniture at a certain valuation, and I answered the letter. If it is preserved among the archives of the house of Swanland, some future young cygnet of that ilk will marvel who the D. Mortomley was that penned such an epistle. Fancy when he knew how we were situated making such an offer. Just as if he believed we had a secret purse."

"He might have imagined your friends would come forward to help at such a crisis," said Mrs. Werner gently.

"I do not think Mr. Swanland's imagination ever took such an erratic flight as that," answered Dolly bitterly.

"Did you see the old place before it was dismantled?" inquired Mrs. Werner. "I suppose not."

"Yes. I had to go over to point out an inlaid desk Mrs. Dean had forgotten in the excitement of her departure. Mr. Dean went to Mr. Swanland and mentioned the omission.

Mr. Swanland said that if Mrs. Dean would call at Homewood and point out the article in question to his man, it should be taken to Salisbury House, there to await Mr. Dean's orders. Mr. Dean thought Mrs. Dean could not possibly go to Homewood in the present unhappy state of affairs. He suggested that 'his wife, etcetera, etcetera,' and Mr. Swanland said,

" 'Quite so; yes, exactly.' Lang, who happened to be in the outer office, heard all this and told me about it.

" Then Mr. Dean and Mr. Swanland both wrote, requesting me to go to Homewood and point out the curiosity, and though very much inclined to say ' No,' still I went."

" Poor dear Dolly! " ejaculated Mrs. Werner, for there was a break in her friend's voice.

" I am glad I went," Mrs. Mortomley went on ; " glad I saw the old home with its death face on. Otherwise, I might in fancy have imagined Homewood still alive, and it is dead. I should tell you that Meadows is no longer Mr. Swanland's lord-lieutenant there. The evening we left Homewood he went out with

some of the men and got drunk, a process he
repeated so often that at the end of a fortnight
he was laid up with what he called inflamma-
tion of the lungs, and had to be carried off the
premises.   Then Mr. Swanland sent down
another man, and that man took his wife into
residence with him, together with five of the
very ugliest children I ever beheld.   They all
squinted horribly—they all followed me about
the place—they all looked at me—' so,' " and
Dolly distorted the axis of her eyes to such an
extent that Mrs. Werner covered hers up and
said,

"Don't, Dolly ; pray, pray, don't.   Think
if your eyes should remain as they are."

"Then they would resemble the eyes of
those nice children," answered Dolly, who, in
the genial atmosphere of Mrs. Werner's presence, seemed to be recovering her temper and
her spirits.   "Do let me tell you all about it,
Lenny.   The   mother   wondered   I   had   not
taken away my beautiful wool-work, evidently
imagining I wrought those wonders of sofa-
pillows and anti-macassars, which so much
impressed her, with my own hand."

" ' The last lady with whom I was,' she said, ' lamented nothing so much as her chairs; they were all done up with wool-work.'

" ' Wasn't theirs forty thousand ?' asked the biggest of the children, with one eye fixed on his mother's face, and the other roaming over the garden.

" ' Yes, dear, it were a big thing,' she said hurriedly, evidently thinking I might feel hurt to know the ' lady ' had been so much greater a personage than myself. ' She was in the public line you see, ma'am,' she went on, ' and the house was just beautiful. She cried about them chairs, she did. She said if she had known how things was a-going to be, she would have got them away anyhow.' And then the wretch went on to say how cheerful that public-house was in comparison with Homewood, and how she did hope they would get back to London before long, and how Mr. Swanland hated dogs; and how our men and their friends had got leave to take one and another, except poor old Lion, who was desired by nobody,—you remember Lion, Nora;

and how she wished to gracious some one would soon take him, for 'the creature was half-starved and so savage no one dare go anigh him.'

"Then I asked how about the fowls and the pigeons and the cat; and the children in chorus told how the fowls were all stolen and the pigeons gone, and the cat so wild she would not come to anybody; and I wanted to get away and cry by myself, Nora, but they would not leave me—no, not for a moment.

"I had caught the braid of my dress on a bramble, and asked the woman to lend me a needle and cotton to run it on again, and when she was looking up those items and a thimble, I saw she had annexed my drawing box to her own use. 'It was a handy box,' she said. Do not imagine I cared for it, Lenny," added Dolly. "Unlike the lady in the public line, I had passed beyond that state in life when one cries for lost wool-work and desecrated girlish treasures."

"Do not go on—do not, Dolly," entreated Mrs. Werner.

"I will," answered Dolly pitilessly. " I have found my tongue and I must speak. I went out and called the cat—called and called, and at last from half a mile distant, as it seemed, the creature answered. I called and she still kept answering till she came in sight, and then, when she beheld those horrid children, she stopped—her tail straight on end, and her ears pricked up.

" 'Stay where you are,' I said to the little wretches, and I went and caught and stroked her, and she rubbed her face against mine, and I felt her poor ribs, and the bones were coming through her skin—oh! Lenny, Lenny, I realized it all then—understood what our ruin meant to us and to the dumb brutes who had trusted to us for kindness."

Mrs. Mortomley laid her head on Mrs. Werner's lap, and sobbed as if her heart would break.

"Lion was wild with hunger," she went on after a pause. " When I unfastened his collar the children fled indoors, frightened lest he should eat them, and, God forgive me, I should

not have cared if he had ; and the horses—I
could not unloose their halters and bring
those poor brutes with me. I can talk about
it no more.

"That day killed me. I do not mean that
I am going to die, or any nonsense of that sort,
but I am not the same Dolly I was—not the
Dolly you knew once—and loved."

Mrs. Werner did not answer. She turned
up Mrs. Mortomley's face and looked at it
through blinding tears—no, not the Dolly of
the olden time, not the Dolly she had loved
so much, but another Dolly who was dearer to
her an hundredfold than any woman she had
ever previously known or ever might know
again—a woman with a soft heart and a great
courage, the bravest, tenderest, truest woman,
woman ever loved.

Like a far-off echo was the love she had
once felt for Mortomley himself. Like the
sound of an air solemn and sweet was the love
she felt for the friend of her youth, Mortomley's wife.

Two fine natures they possessed, those

friends; but the finer, the truer, the loftier nature of the two was, spite of all her short-comings, possessed by the woman who chanced to be in such sore distress, and Mrs. Werner, with her strong intellect, grasped this fact.

"What were the men about," asked Mrs. Werner after a pause, "that they did not see after the animals you left behind?"

"My dear," said Dolly, "have you ever been in a house when the mother just dead has left no one behind to look after the children? I think every one must once in a lifetime have seen how the irresponsible, unruly brats comport themselves. Homewood is in that strait. The men are all at daggers drawn, each wants to be master, each wants to be a gentleman of leisure. There are five foremen and three managers seeing to the work now. Lang has left, or rather Lang has been dismissed."

"Why?" inquired Mrs. Werner.

"It is an old story now, as stories are with us—three weeks old at all events. Some great firm who had never done business with

Archie before, sent to the Thames Street
warehouse for a specimen of that wonderful
blue which he brought out eighteen months
ago, and of course the letter went on to
Salisbury House.

"They knew nothing of the bankruptcy,
and ordered, oh! some enormous quantity of it
to be despatched to America.

"Well, Mr. Swanland sent this order to
Homewood, and Lang went up to his office,
and said plainly the blue could not be made
unless Mr. Mortomley superintended the
manufacture. Hankins went up and said
it could. Lang came to Archie, and Archie
wrote to Mr. Swanland offering to see that the
order was properly executed.

"Mr. Swanland wrote in reply that he would
not trouble Archie personally to superintend
the manufacture, but if he would kindly send
him a memorandum of the process it might be
useful.

"Archie declined to do this. He said he
was quite willing to produce the colour, but
he could not give the formula.

"Mr. Swanland then appealed to Hankins, who said he knew all about the manufacture. Lang said no one knew how to manipulate the materials but Archie, and that Hankins had as much acquaintance with the process needful to ensure success as a donkey with Arithmetic.

"Mr. Swanland seemed to think there was something personal in Lang's utterances, and told him his services could be dispensed with after the following Saturday. Lang claimed a month's notice or four weeks' wages. Mr. Swanland declined to give either Lang threatened to summon him, at which idea Mr. Swanland laughed. Lang then went to a lawyer, who said he could not summon a trustee. Lang said he would do it for the annoyance of the thing, and so threw away half a sovereign which he now repents, because the case cannot come on. He has got another situation, a very good berth as he styles it. He is to have a (for him) large amount of money to go abroad as consulting manager to some great works in course of formation in Germany. One

of the partners is an Englishman, and knew
Lang at a time when he was in business on his
own account. It will be a good thing for him,"
and Dolly sighed heavily.

Good things came to other people, but not
to Mortomley or his wife.

"What a simpleton that Mr. Swanland must
be!" remarked Mrs. Werner.

"For not accepting Archie's offer, I suppose
you mean," suggested Mrs. Mortomley. "I
do not think so. What does he care about the
trade, or the colours, or anything, so long as
he can find work for his clerks, and knock up
a fresh peg in his office on which to hang up
the whole of the estate? Lang says —"

"Dolly dear, I do not care to hear what
Lang says," interrupted Mrs. Werner. "I do
not imagine that the utterances of an *employé*
concerning his employer can be very profitable
under any circumstances."

"Perhaps not," agreed Mrs. Mortomley; but
she sighed again.

"Did you ever get your trunks away from
Homewood," inquired Mrs. Werner, in order to
change the subject.

" Yes," was the short reply.

" Did Mr. Swanland send them to you, or had you to apply for them again, or—"

" Mr. Swanland did not send them to me," said Dolly, as her friend paused. " I applied for them, and he first agreed I should have the boxes, and then thought it was a useless form having them removed from Homewood. So I said nothing more on the subject, and neither did he ; but they are here."

" How did they come ?" asked Mrs. Werner.

" That I cannot tell you. One Sunday evening, when I returned from church, they were piled up in the kitchen. I promised never to say how they were got away or who brought them ; and, indeed, though half tempted to send them back again, I was thankful to have a few decent clothes to wear again once more."

Mrs. Werner looked down at her friend, and smiled as her glance wandered over the pale grey silk dress and black velvet upper skirt and bodice in which Dolly had thought fit to bemoan her lot.

Would Dolly ever be Dolly, she wondered, without her masses of hair—her pretty dresses —her small effects of jewellery—her little graceful knicknacks — and purely feminine deceptions.

No; they were an integral part of my heroine's imperfect character.

Honestly, and to be utterly outspoken, it was a comfort to Dolly, in the midst of her misery, to be able to array herself in purple and fine linen. Poor little soul! wretched though she might be and was, she did not feel herself so completely forsaken by God and man when attired in silk velvet and stiff silk as she might if only in a position to appear in a linsey gown. Vanity shall we say? As you please, my readers. The matter is really of little importance; only allow me to remark, there is a vanity near akin to self-respect—a desire to turn the best side of one's life's shield out for the world to see, which often invests poverty itself with a certain grace of reticence and dignity of non complaint, that we look for in vain amongst those who allow the unmended rags and tatters of their lost prosperity to flaunt in the breeze and stimulate the compassion of every passer-by.

"That reminds me, Dolly," said Mrs. Werner, after a slight pause. "I meant to buy you a Christmas present."

"I am very glad you did not carry out your intention then," retorted Mrs. Mortomley; "for I should not have taken the present."

Mrs. Werner laughed.

"I do not mean to buy it for you, Dolly," she remarked; "but I shall give it to you nevertheless."

"I will not have it," her friend repeated. "I will take nothing from you now, save love and kisses."

"Why, my dear?" asked Mrs. Werner. "In the old days Dolly Gerace would have accepted anything Leonora Trebasson offered her as freely as Leonora Trebasson would have taken Dolly's gift, small or large. What has come between us? What have I done, Dolly, that you should now shut the doors of your heart against me?"

" I have not shut the doors of my heart against you, Lenny, and you are wicked to say anything of the kind," was the reply. " But it is no longer you and me—it is no longer you and me, and your mother and my aunt, but—"

" Finish your sentence, dear," said Mrs. Werner, as Dolly paused, unwilling, in the presence of a man's wife, to terminate her utterance with an ungracious reference to the absent husband.

"There is no necessity," answered Mrs. Mortomley ; "you know what I mean as well as I do myself."

" Let me see if you are right," was the reply, spoken almost caressingly. " You would take anything from me, but you will have nothing from my husband—belonging to or coming from him—directly or indirectly ; is not that your standpoint, Dolly ?"

"Yes," Dolly answered. "I hate to seem ungracious, but I could receive nothing from your hands, knowing you were but the filter through which—"

"Mrs. Mortomley, you are eminently unhappy in your suggestions," said her friend. " We need not pursue your curious metaphor to its inevitable end. It is simply because I am Henry Werner's wife, and because, having no fortune of my own, my money comes from him that you refuse my little present."

"For once, Leonora, you have performed the marriage service over my words and yours, and made the twain one," answered Mrs Mortomley. " To put the case plainly, I could take anything — a dry crust or a hundred thousand pounds from you, but I could not take a sovereign or a sovereign's worth from your husband."

" You mistake my husband, dear. But let that pass ; or, rather, I cannot let it pass ; for I must tell you, if Henry thought you wanted his help, he would be the first to ask me to offer it. Never shake your head, Dolly."

" I won't, Nora, if it vexes you."

" And say to me solemnly, love, that you only object to me because I am Henry Werner's wife ; that you only refuse my present because bought with my husband's money."

"That is true, Lenny. I could refuse nothing that came from you yourself."

"Then, darling, you won't refuse this;" and Mrs. Werner placed in Dolly's hands a tiny little purse and pocket-book bound together in ivory. "Charley, my cousin—you remember Charley—sent me the contents of that purse to buy some little trinket for myself as a memory of the old days at Dassell. He has married an heiress, Dolly; and those waste lands in the north, my uncle was always lamenting over, have turned out to be a sort of El Dorado. Charley's dear kind letter reached me yesterday, and I straightway wrote back to him, saying,

"Besides yourself I never had but one friend in all my life. I wanted ·to make a present to her, and you have supplied the means. Believe me, in granting me the power to do this you have given me ropes of pearls—to quote Lothair—and miles on miles of diamonds; so there it is, dear—poor Charley's Christmas gift to me, of which my husband knows nothing."

And she rose, and fastening her fur cloak would have departed, but that Dolly, clutching her arm, said,

"Don't go, Leonora, for an instant. Let me exorcise my demon with the help of your presence."

"Pride, dear," suggested the other.

"I do not know—I cannot tell. He rends me to pieces, and I hate myself and him. I want your present badly, Lenny, and yet—and yet I long to compel you to take back your gift."

"Darling," answered Mrs. Werner, "though you are a mother, you never knew what it was to have a mother to love you. Fancy, for a moment I am your mother, saying, 'Dolly, keep it.' Could not that reconcile you, love. And some day it may be I or one belonging to me shall in bitter strait need your help; you would not then like to remember you had refused in your trouble to be assisted by one of us. You would not wish now to place a barrier between yourself and any one belonging to me who might hereafter ask your aid."

"No," Dolly answered slowly. "I should not. It may be—impossible as it now seems—that one of your children, or even you yourself, Leonora, might hereafter stand in need of such comfort as I could give; and just as surely as I take your present to-night, I will return your goodness then. In the words of The Book, 'May God do so to me and more if ever for ever I forget you and yours.'"

"Thank you, Dolly, it is a good vow for Christmas Eve. Good-bye dear, do not come out with me."

For reply, Dolly folding a shawl around her walked along the Grove and to the cross road where Mr. Werner's carriage was waiting.

"You ought not to be out in this damp night air," said Mrs. Werner.

But Dolly only shook her head. The footman banged the door, the coachman touched his horses, Mrs. Werner put down the window and waved her hand, and Dolly returned to the small house all alone. There, expecting perhaps to find a ten-pound note in the silken folds of the new purse, she opened Mrs.

Werner's present; but, behold! it was no bank-note which her fingers discovered, but a slip of paper on which was written,

"Pay to Mrs. Werner or order one hundred pounds," and on the back a signature, that of "Leonora Werner."

CHAPTER III.

WHAT MR. LANG THOUGHT.

As Mrs. Werner drove home a cruel pain
seemed tearing her heart to pieces. She had
loved Dolly as child, as girl, as woman, with a
love almost equalling that of a mother. She
had longed for Dolly to be different, desired to
see her grasp life with a firmer hand, and
learn the lessons taught by experience as something
more real than an idle jest. Dolly's
frivolity had chafed her spirit even in the
old Dassell days, but it had vexed her more
since the time of her own marriage.

If she regarded the journey of existence as
a serious affair, what right had Mr. Gerace's
daughter to comport herself along the way as

though she were but one of a picnic party, as though it were always first of May and fine weather with her?

Life should have been just as momentous a business at Homewood as at the West-End, where Henry Werner had set up his domestic gods; but Dolly could never be brought to see the iniquity of her own light-heartedness; and Mrs. Werner, who frequently found the hours and the days pass heavily enough in the ponderous atmosphere of respectability which her husband affected, could often have found it in her heart to box Dolly's ears for her levity of deportment and lightness of heart.

And now Dolly was serious enough, and yet Mrs. Werner felt dissatisfied—more than dissatisfied. She was in despair; the ideal Dolly she had always regarded as possible if not probable; but the frivolous, light-hearted, smiling Dolly she had foolishly desired to change, could never come back with her gay tones, with her laughing face, on this side Heaven.

Could Mrs. Werner at that moment have

caught sight of the former Dolly, she would not have rebuked her for undue merriment.

She might have talked her light, innocent, mocking talk for the length of a summer's day without causing a shade to pass across her friend's face; she might have laughed till the welkin rang, and Mrs. Werner would not have marvelled how she could be so silly; she might have ridiculed all the decorous people within a circle of fifty miles had it pleased her, and Mrs. Werner would never have remarked she feared her powers of mimicry would get her into trouble.

"And I thought myself better than Dolly," considered Mrs. Werner. "Imagined I was a more faithful wife, a higher type of womanhood; I, who could not endure what she has borne so patiently; I, who must have compelled any man, sick or well, to bear the burden with me, who could never forgive any man weak enough or wicked enough to compass such ruin for his wife and family! My dear, the look in your poor face to-night, as you sat with the firelight gleaming upon it, will haunt me till I die."

The result of which meditation was that, the first thing on Christmas morning, Mrs. Werner despatched this note to Dolly by a special messenger,

" I wish, dear, you would give me a Christmas gift,—your promise that so soon as Mr. Mortomley's presence can be dispensed with at Salisbury House, you will go away from town for a short time. I am quite certain your husband will never get well in London, and there can be no doubt but that you require a change almost as much as he does,

With fond love,

Yours,

LEONORA."

To which, detaining the messenger while she wrote, Mrs. Mortomley replied,

" Dear Lenny,—Ere this, you will have received my note written last night concerning your Christmas present, so I need say no more on that subject. But oh ! Lenny, how could you steal such a march upon me ?

" Yes, I will promise what you ask. We

will leave London the moment we can do so, and remain away as long as possible—if it rested with me, for ever. I have no desire to remain here—I shall have none to return here.

Always yours,

DOLLY.

" Rupert dragged Archie about last night with the idea of doing him good, till he was quite exhausted, and the consequence is that he does not feel nearly so well this morning. Good-bye, a merry Christmas to you, my dear, and many, and many happy new years."

For Dolly, whatever the new year might hold in store, she made a very pleasant Christmas for herself and others in that small house at Clapton. Miss Gerace had sent up a hamper filled with farm-house produce to her niece, and that hamper was supplemented by another filled with game shot in Dassell woods.

The three—Rupert, Mortomley and Dolly —consequently sat down to as nice a little dinner as could have been furnished at Elm

Park, whither Rupert was invited to eat turkeys and mince pies. But he preferred for reasons of his own holding high festival with his uncle and aunt, and Dolly rewarded him by proving as gracious and pleasant a hostess in adversity as she had often been in the days of her prosperity.

The change Mrs. Werner beheld had been wrought almost under Rupert's eyes by a process so gradual that it failed to affect him as it had touched her friend.

He saw she grew thinner and paler. He knew she was more silent and thoughtful than of old. He heard her laugh had lost its ringing clearness, and that her smile, once so bright and sunny, had something of a wintry gleam about it, but these changes were but the natural consequence of what she had gone through, the legitimate scars left from wounds received during the course of that weary battle which had been fought out bravely if foolishly to the end.

She could be pleasant and lively enough still, he decided, as she talked and laughed while nibbling like a squirrel as he suggested, the walnuts he prepared for her delectation.

Aye, and she could be wise and strong too, he thought as he met her brown eyes fixed gravely on his, while she solemnly touched his wine-glass with her own, and hoped in a tone, which was almost a prayer, that the coming year might prove a happier and more prosperous one to them all.

She was vexed with Rupert for having allowed and indeed encouraged her husband to over-exert himself, but she was pleased with Rupert for having relinquished the gaieties of Elm Park in their favour.

It is always a pleasant thing for a woman to know or imagine her society is preferred to that of some other woman, even though that other woman should occupy the humble position of a man's sister, and Dolly, much as she loved her husband, did feel gratified that on the occasion of their first Christmas dinner after leaving Homewood, they were not compelled to take that meal *tête-à-tête*.

True, they had invitations by the dozen, but then that was a different matter.

The people who sent those invitations, although they understood Mr. Mortomley was ruined, did not, could not realize the length and breadth, and height and depth of the gulf which divided the Mortomleys of Clapton from the Mortomleys of Homewood.

Now Rupert did understand, and she felt the better pleased with his self-proffered company.

And as he was there she rejoiced that her aunt had sent up so well-stocked a hamper, and she inwardly blessed Lord Darsham for having ordered such a supply of game to be left at Eglantine Cottage ; and she was glad Rupert should see there seemed no lack of anything in their temporary home, small though its limits might be ; and above all she felt thankful for the cheque lying safely in her new purse, which removed such a weight and load of care from her.

" One hundred pounds," she kept mentally repeating to herself, while her heart throbbed joyfully in accord with the air her mind was singing—"Why, one hundred pounds properly

managed—and I do now understand how to
manage money—will last for ever."

Poor Dolly, she was not such a simpleton as
her ideas might lead any one to imagine;
already she had formed her plans for the
future, and Rupert, looking at her sparkling
face, guessed that some good had come to or
was expected by her.

"She would never be so cheerful as she is,"
the young man decided, "with only five
pounds between them and beggary, unless she
had got more or knew where to get it. I will
put my idea to the test presently."

And so, when after dinner and coffee Mortomley had fallen into that evening sleep now
become habitual, and which the doctor told
Dolly to encourage, Rupert drew his chair
near to his companion and said in a low tone,

"Dolly, are you rich enough to lend me
fifteen pounds? I can repay you in a fortnight or three weeks. Of course Dean would
lend me that amount, but then I do not care to
ask a favour from him. Talking about money
to you and Archie never seems the same evil

thing as talking about money to other people."

Dolly looked up at him frankly. "You do not want it to-night, I suppose?"

"No; any time within a few days, will do."

"You can have it on Thursday," she said, "that is if the weather be fine enough for me to go to town, and I shall not want it again at present. You need not repay me for a couple of months if you are short."

"She *has* discovered a gold mine," decided Rupert, but he only said aloud, "Thank you, Dolly, very much. He who gives quickly gives twice, and you always had that grace, my dear."

Next day Mrs. Mortomley had a visitor, one who came when the afternoon was changing into evening, and who sent up a mysterious message to Mrs. Mortomley by Susan to the effect that "a person wanted to speak to her."

"It is Lang, ma'am," whispered Susan, as she followed her mistress across the hall; "but he charged me not to mention his name before Mr. Rupert. He says if you wouldn't mind step-

ping down and speaking to him, he would take
it as a kindness."

When Mrs. Mortomley entered the kitchen,
she beheld Lang standing in front of a bright
fire, his hands crossed behind him, his face
turned towards the darkness closing outside.

" How do you do, ma'am," he began. " I
hope you will excuse the liberty, but I leave
to-morrow, and I felt I could not go without
just mentioning that matter to you again."

Mrs. Mortomley at the first glance understood Mr. Lang had been drinking—paying
his last footing for a time on English soil, and
toasting prosperity to number one in a foreign
land. But this made no difference in the
cordiality of her reception—sober or not sober,
and she had seen him in both states, she
knew Lang could speak to the purpose. That
unhappy glass too much which overtakes the
best and cleverest of our skilled labourers on
occasion, was not so rare an accident in Mr.
Lang's life that Dolly feared any forgetfulness
of etiquette in consequence.

" Pray sit down," she said, pointing to a

chair, and then she would have drawn down the blind and lit the gas had not Lang prevented her.

"I think I can do that much at any rate," he remarked; but whether his observation had a special or a particular application, Dolly was unable to tell.

It appeared, however, as though he was able to do "that much," for he lit the gas and drew down the blinds, and then placed a seat for Mrs. Mortomley.

"If you will excuse me, ma'am," he said, "but I believe it is as cheap to sit as to stand."

"Certainly it is," agreed Dolly, and accepted the proffered civility, Mr. Lang seating himself on the other side of the hearth.

"Yes, I am going away to-morrow," repeated Mr. Lang, with that harking back, without a previous link to a first idea, which is so curious a peculiarity of his class.

"I hope you will make a great success," said Dolly. With the peculiarity of her class, she was able to appear utterly indifferent, while her heart was aching till she heard Lang's next words.

"I shall make some money, of that I have no doubt," answered the man. "I have the knowledge, and knowledge is what people want now-a-days; but, bless you, I know what they'll do—they'll pick my brains and then throw me aside like a sucked orange," he finished, with a singular involvement of metaphor.

Mrs. Mortomley did not answer. She had some knowledge of his class, derived from that insight which a clever woman who personally relieves those who make their living by labour, when they are sick or distressed, must acquire almost unconsciously, and she did not wish to lose a point in her game by precipitancy.

"Like a sucked orange as that blackguard Swanland would have liked to do," Mr. Lang kindly explained.

"I suppose you will start in business on your own account when you return to England," said Mrs. Mortomley, seeing some reply was expected from her.

" No," answered Mr. Lang slowly and solemnly ; " no, no, that ain't good enough for me, not by no means. If I can earn enough in foreign parts (I want no secrets from a lady like you) I will put the wife into a business. That there new Act is a jolly good thing for such as us ; and then, if you have no call for me, I'll try to get a berth as foreman. Mrs. Mortomley," he added almost in a whisper, and bending his head eagerly forward, " *have you found anything yet ?* "

" No," she answered ; " nevertheless, I think it is to be done. Lang," and rising in her earnestness she went on, " are you true or are you false ? Can I trust you or can I not ? "

" True before God, ma'am," he replied rising likewise. " And you may trust me to the death."

" That is enough," she answered ; then added imperatively, " Sit down. If you are going to-morrow, I must speak to you now."

" Is—is there a drop of cold tea about anywhere, ma'am ? " he asked, feeling he needed something perfectly to steady his senses, and yet fearing to touch water as though he were a mad dog.

Dolly laughed; the experience tickled her, and going to a cupboard which held Susan's treasures, produced a pot from which she poured a cup of cold tea.

"Milk and sugar?" she asked.

"Milk will do, thank you," said Mr. Lang, and he drank half a pint off at a draught.

Mrs. Mortomley watched him finish with a grave smile; then she said,

"If you and I are ever to row in the same boat, Lang, you must take less—cold tea."

"I'd take the pledge if you asked me," he answered eagerly, but Dolly shook her head.

"Whenever Mr. Mortomley has to attend no longer at Salisbury House," she said, "I mean to leave London."

"Well, our work can be done anywhere," said Lang reflectively.

"That is precisely what I think," agreed Mrs. Mortomley; "but before we go further I want you to understand one thing clearly. Through misadventure I am not going to sell

my husband a second time. If I ever find
those formulæ, or if I am ever able to extract
them from Mr. Mortomley's memory, I shall
keep them to myself. Do you understand?
If you like to work with me on that condition,
well and good; if not, let us wish each other
fortune's best gifts, and part now, you to go to
Germany, I to do the best I can in England."

Mr. Lang paused. This was a move he had
not expected; but aided, perhaps, by the cold
tea, he recovered himself immediately.

"I am quite willing to work with you and
for you, ma'am, on those conditions. If I
serve you faithful, I am sure you won't leave
my name out when your books are balanced.
Look here, ma'am, I did think to go in with
you share and share alike in everything,
but—"

"Look *you* here, Lang," Mrs. Mortomley
interrupted, speaking very decidedly, "My
husband's brains are all that are left to him
now, and I will help no man to steal them,
neither will I suffer any one to steal them, you
may depend. I am thankful to remember Mr.

Swanland when he took his business from him, was unable to take his trade secrets as well, and I will put it in the power of no person to use Mr. Mortomley's processes without his knowledge and permission. So now, as I said before, if you do not like my conditions, let us abandon your plan. About money, if we make any, I shall not be niggardly; but if you stay with me for twenty years, you will know no more of Mr. Mortomley's secrets than you do to-night."

Lang sat silent for a minute. He had not bargained for this. He had felt willing enough to prosecute the plan he himself had suggested to Mrs. Mortomley without any immediate re-velations being made to him concerning the manipulation of those choicer colours for which the Mortomleys had long been famous, but he was not prepared for the frank assurance that Mrs. Mortomley intended to leave him out in the cold for ever. He intended to be utterly true to the Mortomleys; but, at the same time, he desired naturally to serve himself, and he believed he could never hope to do that effectually unless he were made acquainted with the means whereby his late employer had produced those effects which rendered the Homewood works celebrated wherever colours were bought and sold.

Who would have supposed that a lady who twelve months before could not have told ochre from umber should all at once develope such an amount of business capacity as to understand precisely which way Mr. Lang's desires led, and at once put a padlock on the gate by which he hoped to reach his goal?

Mr. Lang sat and thought this over as thoroughly as the state of his head would permit, and Dolly sat and watched him anxiously. She was determined not to yield a point; and yet if Lang decided to have nothing to do with those still unopened works, the idea of which had been originated by himself, she failed to see what she should unaided be able to accomplish.

At last Lang spoke. "I think you are hard upon me, ma'am. If I do my best to work up a business for Mr. Mortomley, it seems only justice I should have some benefit from it."

"That is quite true," agreed Mrs. Mortomley.

"But I cannot have any tangible benefit unless— "

"Go on," said Dolly as he paused, "or shall I finish the sentence for you—unless we take you so far into our confidence that we could not safely throw you over."

"I do not think, ma'am, you ought to put it in that way," remarked Lang, who naturally disliked such explicit utterances.

"If you can suggest any better way in which to put it, pray do so," she replied. "The fact is, Lang, one or other of us must have faith—you in me, or I in you. Now I think it is you who ought to have faith in me, because so far as anything is mine to trust, you shall have perfect control over it. I must put the most utter confidence in your honesty, your skill, and your industry. The only trust I withhold is that which is not mine to give, which belongs entirely to my husband;

but this much I will say, Lang,—if hereafter, when Mr. Mortomley's health is re-established, differences should arise among us, and you desire to leave, I would most earnestly ask him to mark his sense of all you have done and tried to do for me by giving you two or three receipts, which might enable you to carry on a small business successfully on your own account."

" You would do that, ma'am ? "

" Most certainly," she answered.

" Would you mind giving me your hand on it ? "

Dolly laughed, and held out her hand. What a bit of a hand it was ! Mr. Lang took it in his as he might have taken a fragile piece of china, and appeared excessively uncomfortable now he had got what he desired.

" There is one thing more I would wish to say, ma'am," he remarked, when, this ceremony concluded, an awkward pause seemed impending.

" Why do you not say it then ? " asked Mrs. Mortomley.

"Because I am afraid of offending. But I may just observe that I hope you won't think of making Mr. Rupert one of our firm."

"Mr. Rupert!" she repeated in surprise. "He has done with business for ever. He would never wish to be connected with it again."

"But if he did, ma'am?"

"I should not wish it," Mrs. Mortomley answered. Then added, "I would not have Mr. Rupert in any business in which I had any interest. I am certain he would do his best to serve me or his uncle, but I do not think he has any especial genius for colour making."

"They do say at Swanland's," observed Mr Lang, coughing apologetically, "that there is a great talk of Mr. Rupert going into business with Mr. Brett. They do say there Mr. Rupert knows all Mr. Mortomley's processes; and if so be as how such is the case, Mr. Brett and he will make a good thing of it."

Dolly sat silent for a minute; then she asked,

"Did Mr. Rupert know anything of the

business when we were at Homewood,
Lang."

"No, that I will take my oath he did not,"
was the prompt reply.

"Then by what means could he have
learned anything of it since?"

"That is best known to himself, ma'am.
If he found anything at Homewood, and kept
it—"

"He could not, Lang. My husband was
always most careful about his papers."

"Or if he has been able to pump Mr. Mortomley since you left Homewood."

"That is not likely either," said Dolly, and
yet as she spoke she remembered that not five
minutes before Susan came·to tell her Lang
was below, her husband had thrust a piece of
paper over to Rupert, saying, "There is something out of which money might be made,
though I shall never make it," and like a
simpleton she had attached little importance to
the utterance, until Lang's words revealed its
significance to her.

"Suppose we leave Mr. Rupert out of the
question altogether," she suggested.

"Well, ma'am, I don't see how that can well be, if Mr. Rupert is to get the information we want and use it against us," Lang replied.

"He shall not," was the reply. "He may have caught a hint or two, but he shall catch no more. If he and Mr. Brett go into partnership, it shall not be with Mr. Mortomley's inventions."

"Are you sure, ma'am?"

"Perfectly sure. Mr. Mortomley is not in a state of health to detail the methods he has employed to any one. I do not mean to say Mr. Rupert may not have got some information, but I do say he would require as much more to make it available, and I will take care he has no chance of obtaining any more."

"I hope you will, ma'am," was the frank reply, "for if I may make so free as to give you my opinion about Mr. Rupert, I think, fine young gentleman as he is, he would sell the nearest belonging to him for a ten pound-note."

" You have no right to say anything against Mr. Rupert," answered Mrs. Mortomley, "and there is no necessity for you to express any opinion concerning him. He will have nothing to do with our business, and therefore you need not trouble yourself about his character.

" I meant no offence, ma'am."

" And I have taken none, but I want to talk to you about business, and we are wasting time in speaking of extraneous matters. When shall you come back to England ? "

" Whenever you want me."

" But you have certain work to finish abroad ? "

" That is true ; still, I can take a run over when you are ready to start our work. We shall have a good deal to prepare before we can begin in earnest, and I shall set a man I can depend on to do all that, and have everything ready for me by the time I am clear. You find the place, ma'am, and the money, and we need not delay matters an hour."

" Want of money is no obstacle now," she

answered. "I can give you enough at any time."

"And where do you think of going?" he asked.

"Into Hertfordshire if I can find a house cheap enough. I shall look for the house first, and the shed you require afterwards."

"Remember, we must have water," he said. "Good water and a continuous supply."

"I shall not forget," was the reply.

"And you think you can find the memoranda?"

"I do not think I can. I think that from time to time I may be able to obtain all particulars from Mr. Mortomley."

Lang groaned. "You do not know, ma'am, on what a trifle success hangs in the colour trade. If you could only have got hold of the receipts the governor wrote out when he was at his best—"

"I do not believe he ever wrote out any," said Mrs. Mortomley."

"He must have done it," was the reply. "No memory, let it be good as might be, could carry things like that."

"If there had been a book such as you suppose, it would have gone up to Salisbury House with the rest of my husband's books and papers. If it ever existed Mr. Swanland has it."

"I don't think it, ma'am. If Mr. Swanland knows nothing except about accountants' work, he has those in his employ who would have understood the value of such a book as that."

"Good heavens!" exclaimed Dolly pettishly. "Do you suppose any one in Mr. Swanland's office ever waded through the mass of papers Meadows sent up to town? Why, there were tons of letters, and books and papers, in the offices at Homewood."

"That may well be," agreed Lang; "but Mr. Mortomley never kept his secrets among the office papers. Had he not desks and writing-tables, and the like?"

"Yes; but we left everything in them untouched. I should have liked to look over the papers after Meadows came, but I was afraid to meddle with them."

"Well, it cannot be helped," remarked the man resignedly. "Mayhap, by the time we are ready, Mr. Mortomley will be able to help us; if not, we must depend on the colours I know something about."

And having uttered this consolatory reflection, Mr. Lang arose to depart.

"I expect I'll have to be backwards and forwards," he observed; "and if I am, I'll call to know how things are going on; but if not, you'll write, ma'am."

"I will write," she answered; and so they separated.

Thinking it possible her husband might have fallen asleep, Mrs. Mortomley, when she went upstairs, opened the drawing-room door so gently that no one heard her enter.

At a glance she saw her husband, though awake, was lost in reverie, and that Rupert was copying the formula Mortomley had written out into his pocket-book.

"What are you so busy about, Rupert?" she asked, startling him by her question.

He turned a leaf over rapidly and answered,

" Making a sketch of Archie in a ' brown study.' "

" When you come to the accessories of the drawing, let me fill them in," she suggested, lifting the paper as she spoke from the table and looking Rupert steadily in the face.

" I have no doubt you would do so better than I," he replied with imperturbable composure. "A woman's imagination is always so much livelier than that of a man."

She made no reply to this. She only folded up the formula and placed it carefully beside Mrs. Werner's cheque in the pretty purse her friend had given her.

CHAPTER IV.

MORTOMLEY'S BLUE.

THE new year brought with it much glorification of spirit to the manager of St. Vedast Wharf and the two men whose fortunes were, to a certain extent, associated with the temporary success of the General Chemical Company Limited.

Never before had so satisfactory a balance-sheet been presented to the shareholders of that company,—never before had a good dividend been so confidently recommended,—never had accountants audited accounts so entirely satisfactory, or checked securities so stamped with the impress of solvency,—never had the thanks of every one been so due to any body of directors as on that special occasion, and never had any manager, secretary, and the other officers of any company been so efficient, so self-denying, so hard-working, and so utterly conscientious as the manager and other officers connected with that concern which was travelling as fast to ruin as it knew how.

The way in which these things are managed might puzzle even a man experienced in City ways to explain, since each company has its own modes of cooking its accounts and hood-winking the public. But these things are done,—they were yesterday, they have been to-day, they will be to-morrow; and if you live so long, my dear reader, you will hear more about yesterday's doings, and to-day's, and to-morrow's when, a few years hence, you peruse the case of Blank *v.* Blank, or Blank *v.* the Blank Company Limited, or any other improving record of the same sort.

The worst of the whole matter is that our clever financiers always keep a little in advance of the law, as our clever thieves always keep a little in advance of our safemakers.

The gentlemen of a hundred schemes complacently fleece their victims, and Parliament— wise after—says in solemn convocation that the British sheep shall never be shorn in such and such a way again with impunity

Nevertheless, though not in the same way, the sheep is shorn daily, and the shearer escapes scot-free with the wool. Always lagging behind the wit of the culprit comes the wit of the law. It is only the poor wretches who have no brains to enable them to take a higher flight than picking pockets that really suffer.

"You are a hardened ruffian," says the judge, looking through his spectacles at the pickpocket who has been convicted about a dozen times previously, "and I mean to send you for five years where you can pick no more pockets," which indeed the hardened ruffian— stripping off all the false clothing philanthropists love to deck him with—deserves most thoroughly. But, then, what about the hardened ruffians who are never convicted, who float their bubble companies and rob the widow and the orphan as coolly as Bill Sykes, only with smiling faces and well-clothed persons ?

It is unfair, no doubt, these should escape as they do scot-free, and yet I must confess time has destroyed much of my sympathy with the widow and the orphan who entrust their substance to strangers and believe in the possible solvency—for such as them—of twenty per cent. One is growing particularly tired of that countryman, so familiar to Londoners, who loses his money because two total strangers ask if he has faith enough to trust one or the other with a ten-pound-note, and it is difficult to help feeling that a sound flogging judiciously administered to one of these yokels who take up so much of a magistrate's time, would impress the rural mind throughout England much more effectually than any number of remarks from his Worship or leaders in the daily papers.

As one grows older, one's intolerance towards dupes is only equalled by one's intolerance towards bores. A man begins by pitying a dupe and ends by hating him ; and the reason is that a dupe has so enormous a capacity for giving trouble and so great a propensity for getting into it.

At that especial half-yearly meeting, however, of which mention has been made, there were very few dupes connected with the General Chemical Company, Limited. All the new shareholders indeed, and a very small proportion of the old might, it is true, have faith in the concern, but as a rule the directors and the shareholders, the accountants and the officials, knew the whole affair was a farce, got up for the purpose of inducing the general public to invest their money in a concern with which those privileged to peep behind the scenes were most heartily disgusted.

Like many other debts of lesser magnitude, Mortomley's had not yet been entered as bad. His account was kept open, in order that the ample dividend promised by Mr. Swanland at the meeting of creditors might be duly entered to his credit. Meanwhile his unpaid acceptances were still skilfully manipulated as securities, thus:—On one side the books, that everything might be done strictly and in order, appeared the entry, " Bills returned, so much, interest thereon, so much," very little interest being charged, the reader may be certain ; and on the other, " Bills retained, so much," which really made the bankrupt's apparent debt to the concern when a balance was struck something merely nominal.

On the same principle, when a dividend of six per cent. for the half year was recommended, as the profit, admirable in itself, had the slight disadvantage of existing in paper instead of hard cash, the amount required was paid out of capital—" loaned out of capital," as Mr. Forde cleverly defined the transaction ; and next day the shares were quoted in the ' Times ' at a premium, and those most interested in the concern shook hands and congratulated themselves that the meeting had gone off so well.

In fact, the worse trade chanced to be at St. Vedast Wharf, the more it behoved those connected with the establishment to put the best face on affairs, and, to their credit be it spoken, they did. Indeed, but for the revelations of clerks and the sour looks of certain bankers when the Chemical Company was mentioned, even City folks would have had but a very vague idea of the struggle St. Vedast Wharf had to maintain in order to keep itself above water. Poor **Mr.** Forde knew most about that struggle, and so did those unfortunates who were desperately holding on by the piles of the rotten structure in order to escape drowning; but, though none of them realized the fact, it was just as true that St. **Vedast** Wharf could not go on keeping up false appearances for ever—as Mortomley had found it, that to carry on a business with men in possession was not a game capable of indefinite prolongation.

As Mr. Kleinwort had prophesied, the colour works at Homewood were eventually stopped with a suddenness for which no one connected either with the manufacturing or liquidating part of the business was at all prepared. All in a hurry Mr. Swanland summoned a meeting of the Committee, and informed them that as he could no longer carry on the works with a reasonable hope of profit, he thought the best thing which could be done would be to sell off the stock, advertise the lease of the premises for sale, and offer the goodwill of the business to competition.

All of which Mr. Forde naturally opposed; but his being the only dissentient voice amongst the members of the Committee, all of whom had long ago become perfectly sick of Mortomley's Estate, and Mortomley's affairs, the course recommended by the trustee was decided upon.

" What dividend are you going to give us then ?" asked the man who had put so " good a thing " in Mr. Swanland's way.

" Impossible to tell till we see what the stock fetches," was the reply.

" But surely out of the profits of working the business, you can declare a first dividend ? My directors would be very much pleased to see something tangible out of the concern," remonstrated Mr. Forde ; hearing which the opposition colour maker laughed, and said,

"No doubt they would," and Mr. Swanland declared the whole statement about profit and so forth had been an imposition. He would not say any person had wilfully deceived him, but the more he saw of the Homewood works, the more fully he felt satisfied they had never returned anything except a loss.

It was all very well to represent the profit on goods sent out as large—no doubt it was large apparently; but when those goods came to be returned on hand with freight and dock charges, and law charges, and Heaven only knew what besides, the profit became a loss.

That was his, Mr. Swanland's, experience; and, of course, as Mr. Swanland's management could not be supposed other than perfect, his experience was generally accepted as correct. When he said Mortomley could never have made a sixpence out of the concern, creditors shook their heads, and said,

"Ah! that is how our money went," as if legitimate business was some sort of game, at which any man in his senses would continue to play if he were not making a profit out of it.

However, the trustee who understands his business, always hints that his client is either a rogue or a fool. It is safer, perhaps, to imply the latter, because in that case the trustee obtains credit for kindliness of feeling; but there may be occasions on which it is necessary to speak more strongly, and this proved to be one of them.

That unhappy Mortomley had given up everything he possessed on earth, except his own and his wife's wearing apparel, to Mr. Swanland, acting for the debtor and the creditors, and still Mr. Swanland was not satisfied.

Which was particularly hard, seeing the creditors were far from charmed with either Mortomley or his trustee, and that Mortomley, who had once hoped to pay everybody, and retain Homewood, was less charmed still.

Why Mortomley felt dissatisfied has been explained. Why the creditors were dissatisfied can easily be understood, when it is stated that as week after week passed away, their hopes of a dividend grew less and less.

At first, when they repaired to Mr. Swanland's office for information concerning a dividend, they asked "when?" but afterwards they began to ask "what?" And thus, by easy degrees, they were let down to "never," and " nothing."

This was usually the case at Asherill's, except when the risk of a company chanced to be unlimited, and the contributaries solvent, or when a company was limited, and the shares had not been so fully paid up but that the promoters, and the advertising agent, and the liquidator, and the lawyers could afford to leave, perhaps, threepence in the pound for other creditors.

Given a private estate, and it generally came out from Asherill's clear of meat as a picked bone. For this pleasing comparison I am, indeed, indebted to an expression used in Salisbury House.

" We have been rather slack lately," said a

clerk jubilantly, "but we have got a meaty bone now."

And why should the young fellow not have been jubilant? Before Calcraft retired from that profession which he so much adorned, he was pleased doubtless to know a man had been sentenced to be hung by the neck till he was dead.

There is a pleasing adaptability about human nature which enables it to forget the possible pain the gratification of its own pleasure may involve to its fellow-creature; and there can be no question but that Mr. Swanland regarded, and perhaps reasonably, the insane struggles of victims, who felt the hooks of liquidation troublesome, as Calcraft might the mad fight of a criminal against the needful pinioning which enabled matters to go off so decently and quietly about eight o'clock on certain Monday mornings in his memory.

Nevertheless, and though he, at all events, must have had his innings out of Mortomley's estate, Mr. Swanland felt disgusted at the result of his own management of the affair.

Not because he had failed to pay the creditors even a farthing in the pound. To do Mr. Swanland strict justice, he looked upon creditors as he looked upon a debtor, namely, as natural enemies. He hated a debtor because the debtor's creditors gave him trouble, and he hated creditors because they gave him trouble; therefore he was, putting so much personal profit in the bankrupt scale, able to hold the beam straight, and declare both bankrupt and creditor to be equally obnoxious.

Mr. Swanland was a just man, and therefore conscientiously he could not declare the beam fell in favour of disliking one more than the other. He disliked them equally, when each had served his purpose, and he wished to throw both aside. The trustee's reason for feeling disgusted with Mortomley's estate was a very simple one. He had not made out of it what he expected. He had netted nothing like the amount he conceived was to be realised with good management.

Not that he feared a loss, *bien entendu,*— such an error had never yet been written in

the books of Salisbury House; but he knew
he had done that which touched his professional pride almost as keenly. He had
lost profit. He had felt so certain of himself and the *employés*, and the works and
the customers; he had entertained so genuine
a contempt for Mortomley's intellect; such
a profound distrust of his capacity to transact
the simplest business matter in a business
manner; that he really believed when he took
the management of the Homewood works upon
himself that he had the ball at his feet.

Visions even of paying a dividend may have
been vouchsafed to him. Certainly some ex-
traordinary hallucination at one time held him
in thrall, for after he had pocketed considerable sums of money, he actually returned
much of it freely in the shape of wages to
Mortomley's Estate.

There were those who said Mr. Swanland,
finding himself doing so glorious a trade, had
serious thoughts of buying in the plant at
Homewood, with a view of pursuing the
amusement of colour-making in his harmless

moments. Be this as it may, he really had felt very proud of his success, and readily fell into the habit of speaking of Mortomley as a poor creature who did not understand the slightest detail of his own business.

Probably, his culminating hour of triumph was that which brought to Salisbury House the order for Mortomley's New Blue which Dolly mentioned to Mrs. Werner. He was like a child in his personal glorification.

"If I had only leisure to attend to such matters fully, see what a trade I could build up," he said to the opposition colour-maker; "poor Mortomley never had any transactions with this firm, and ere my management of affairs is three months' old I have this letter."

"But still, you must remember, it was Mortomley who made the colour," remarked his opponent, who felt a certain *esprit de corps* and longed to do battle for his order when he heard a man, whom amongst his intimate friends he concisely referred to as "that fool of an accountant," undervaluing those productions he personally would have given something considerable to know how to manipulate.

"Oh! anybody can make a colour," observed Mr. Swanland, who had been turning out Brunswick Greens, Prussian Blues, Chrome Reds, and Spanish Browns with a celerity and a success which fairly overpowered his reason.

"Perhaps so," agreed the other, who certainly felt no desire to see Mortomley reinstated at Homewood. "At the same time, it may be well for you to be cautious about that New Blue; Mortomley never sent out much of it, and you might drop a lot of money if anything should happen to go wrong."

"Pooh!" returned Mr. Swanland, "nothing can go wrong—nothing ever has gone wrong."

With reference to which remark, Henry Werner, when the story was repeated to him, —for it was repeated to every one interested in Mortomley's Estate who had sufficient knowledge of the trade to appreciate Mr. Swanland's humorous thoughts on the subject of colour-making—observed that there was an old saying about "a pitcher going once too often to the well."

With respect to Mortomley's Blue, Mr.
Swanland certainly had perilled the pitcher
containing his profits. To Salisbury House
there came an awful experience in the shape
of one of the partners in the large firm that
had sent the great order which lifted Mr.
Swanland to the seventh heaven of self-glorifi-
cation.

No letter could have sufficed to express the
wrath felt by the principals in the house
of Miller, Lennox, and Co. when they heard
from their correspondents abroad, enclosing a
sample of the " Blue " Mr. Swanland had forwarded to them ; no manager or clerk could,
they knew, be trusted to utter their sentiments
in the matter, and accordingly Mr. Miller himself, after having first called at the Thames
Street warehouse and been referred thence to
Basinghall Street, entered the offices of
Messrs. Asherill and Swanland in a white
heat.

Never, he declared, never in the forty years
he had been in business had so utterly dis-
graceful a transaction come under his notice.

All in vain Mr. Swanland explained,—all in vain he blustered,—in vain Mr. Asherill entreated Mr. Miller to be reasonable, that gentleman stuck to his point.

"There," he said, laying one packet on the table, "is the blue we ordered,—there is the blue you sent."

"And a very good blue too ; I see no difference between them," retorted Mr. Swanland.

"Good God ! sir, don't you know the difference between Prussian Blue and Mortomley's Blue ? Have you been managing a colourworks even for a month, and mean to say you are unaware that Mortomley's Blue is the very best blue ever made ? Why, if we had a clerk who made such a confession I would bundle him neck and crop out of the office."

"You forget, sir, I am not a maker of colours ; I am an accountant," suggested Mr. Swanland with dignity.

"Then why don't you stick to your accounts, and leave the making of colours to some one who does understand his trade ? I suppose this is a fresh development of that precious egg, the new Bankruptcy Act, laid by a lot of astute scoundrels in the City and hatched by a parcel of old women in the House of Commons. Heaven help Mortomley if he has put his affairs into such hands as yours say I. That stuff," and he contemptuously indicated Mr. Hankins' blue, " is on its way back, and you may make the best of it ; one farthing we shall never pay you, and you may consider yourselves fortunate that, in consideration of your gross ignorance, I refrain from instructing our solicitors to proceed against you for damages."

"It is all very well to say you will not pay," Mr. Swanland was beginning, when the other interrupted him with,

"Pay, sir! I will never pay. You may carry the case to the House of Lords if you like,—you may leave the goods at the Docks till the charges amount to treble their original value, and still whistle for your money. All I trust is this may prove a lesson to you not to meddle in affairs of which you evidently understand a little less than my five-year-old grandson."

And having made this statement, he walked out of the office, and in the mental books of Miller, Lennox, and Co. there stands at the present moment a black cross against **Mr.** Swanland's name. A black cross quite undeserved as regarded the matter of the blue. In his soul Mr. Swanland did believe the order had been executed as given; he had trusted to the integrity of Hankins in making the blue, and to the honour of Messrs. Miller and Lennox about paying for it, and his soul sank within him at sound of Mr. Miller's parting words.

To make matters easier, Mr. Asherill, who had been an interested auditor, remarked in a Commination-service sort of tone, "I advised you to have nothing to do with Mortomley's affairs, but, as usual, you disregarded my advice."

Hearing that, Mr. Swanland turned from the window where in a make-believe convivial fashion he had been conversing with himself and his liver, and said, "Shut up."

" *I beg your pardon,*" remarked Mr. Asherill all in italics, " what did you observe ? "

He really thought his ears must have deceived him.

" I did not observe anything ; I asked you to shut up unless you could find something pleasanter to say to a fellow worried as I am than 'I told you so.' "

Mr. Asherill had, of course, long ceased playing whist, nevertheless he at that moment marked " one " against that perfect gentleman —his young partner.

CHAPTER V.

MR. SWANLAND'S CRUMPLED ROSE-LEAF.

THAT unlucky American order proved the worst blow Mr. Swanland had ever received. It hurt his purse, his pride, and his personal affection, since, let him scold Hankins as much as he chose—and he did choose to make a vast number of unpleasant remarks to that person before he discharged him with contumely and without notice ; let him load his last man in possession with reproaches, and assure him that the next time such a thing occurred he should leave his employment instantly ; let him express an opinion that Mortomley deserved to be sent to prison because he refused to divulge the secrets of his trade,—he could not blind himself to the fact that the annoyance was really attributable to his own utter incompetence and presumption; that he had made a fatal mistake when he supposed a manufacturing business was as easy to manage as he had found it to realise the stock-in-trade of a publican, or to dispose of the watches and rings and bracelets of a jeweller in course of liquidation. Nevertheless, it was a comfort to rail against Mortomley, and he railed accordingly.

"If he had fallen in the hands of any other trustee in London, I believe he would have found himself in custody ere this," observed Mr. Swanland, venting his indignation and praising his clemency in the same sentence. "The idea of a man withholding information likely to prove of benefit to his creditors!"

"Shocking!" agreed Kleinwort, to whom he made the remark. "Shocking! but why, dear creature, give you not this so tiresome blackguard to the police? They would take from you and him all trouble; perhaps you feel fear though of the little woman, is it so?"

"Thank Heaven I am afraid of nobody," retorted Mr. Swanland; "that is more I expect than some of your friends could say."

"Very like, my friends are not all as you; there are some great scoundrels in this England of yours." With which parting shot Kleinwort waddled off, leaving the trustee with the feeling that he had been making game of his calamity.

And, in truth, Mr. Swanland could have borne the pecuniary loss (of profit) Mortomley's Blue entailed upon him with much greater equanimity than the ridicule he was compelled to bear in consequence.

The story got wind, as such stories do, and was made the basis of a series of those jokes at which City men laugh, as a child laughs when its nurse bids it do so at her uplifted finger.

He heard about blue till he hated the sight and name of the colour. He was asked how he felt after that "rather blue transaction."

One man accosting him in the street remarked he looked a little blue,—another inquired if he was in the blues; when the Prussians were named in his presence, some one cried out, "Hush! Prussians are a sore subject just now with Swanland."

These pleasantries Mr. Swanland tried at first to carry off lightly. "You mistake," he explained in answer to the last observation, "Prussian Blue is not a sore subject with me, though I admit bronze may be."

"You are quite sure it is not brass, Swanland?" suggested a young fellow, adjusting his eyeglass at the same time, in order to survey the trustee more accurately.

"No," was the reply, "I have plenty of that I am thankful to say."

"You have cause for thankfulness," remarked the other, "for in your profession you must require a good stock of the article."

Altogether, what with questions about the colour of his children's eyes, observations to the effect that no doubt he would take his "annual trip this year inland, to a green

country, instead of the sea, the deep blue sea,"
—remarks that he would be certain to bet on
Cambridge, as their colour must be least
inoffensive, and various other witticisms of the
same kind, which by the force of mere iteration
finally grew amusing to listeners,—the unfortunate trustee's life became a weariness to him.

In his chamber he cursed Mortomley, and a
bird of the air carried the tidings to Mr.
Asherill, who in one and the same breath
rebuked his junior for profanity, and excused
his profanity upon account of the unfortunate
impetuosity of youth.

"You had better conciliate Mortomley,"
said the senior partner, "and induce him to
make this waste stuff valuable. I have no
doubt he is clever enough to help you through,
and that he would do so for a five-pound-
note."

Acting upon which hint, Mr. Swanland upon
some trumpery pretence requested Mortomley's
presence at his office, and having got him
there he placed a little parcel open upon the
table and said,

"By the bye, Mr. Mortomley, I have been asked if you could manufacture a few tons of a colour such as that into your new blue."

Mortomley never even touched the sample before him, though he answered at once,

"No, I could not."

"But you have not examined it, sir," expostulated Mr. Swanland.

"I do not want to examine it," was the reply, "the colour is dry. Do you suppose, for a moment, it is possible to do anything with a colour after it has dried?"

Now Mr. Swanland had supposed it was quite possible to do so, and therefore entreated Mr. Mortomley to look closely at the parcel lying before him.

"What is it?" asked the trustee.

"It is very inferior Prussian blue," was the reply, "and if your friend have, as you say, got a few tons of it, he had better make it up into balls, and sell it to the wholesale houses that supply the oil shops, which in turn supply the laundresses. Ball blue is all it is fit for."

That unhappy Mortomley could not have

made a less fortunate reply had he studied the subject for a week. Mr. Swanland's patience had been so exercised with allusions to the getting up of his linen; offers to give him the names and addresses of washerwomen who might buy a pound or two of blue if he allowed a liberal discount; inquiries as to whether he had not been obliged to apply for a few policemen to keep the staircase at Salisbury House clear for ladies of the washtub persuasion, who had heard of the great bargains Asherill and Swanland were offering in colours, that the slightest allusion to a laundress now affected him as a red rag does a turkey cock.

" You are pleased to be facetious," he observed in a tone which caused Mortomley to turn round and stare at the trustee, while he answered,

"Facetious! there is nothing to be facetious about in the matter. I should say, if your friend have a lot of this wretched stuff thrown on his hands, he must consider the affair something beyond a joke."

Mr. Swanland took a short walk up and

down his office, then, the better apparently for this exercise, he paused and said,

"That wretched stuff, as you call it, was made at Homewood."

Mortomley sat silent for a moment before he remarked,

"I am very sorry to hear it."

"You are not, sir," retorted Mr. Swanland.

"I am," was the reply. "Do you suppose I lost all care for my own trade reputation when, unfortunately, part of it was given over to your keeping?"

And the two men, both now standing, looked straight and dangerously the one at the other.

"Come, Mr. Mortomley," said Mr. Swanland at last, breaking the spell by withdrawing his eyes, in the same fashion as inquisitive folks in Ireland used to be compelled to turn their gaze from the Leprauchaun, "we need not bandy hard words about this unfortunate business, though, I must say, you are the first bankrupt in whose affairs I ever had any concern, who refused to assist me to the extent of his power."

"I have not refused to assist you," was the reply; "on the contrary. You, however, preferred my men to me, and you have reaped the fruits of your preference, that is all."

"That is not all," said Mr. Swanland, "you were bound to make over your formulæ to me."

"I think not," was the reply. "I do not profess to know much of this new law by virtue of which I have been stripped of everything, and my creditors have not been benefited to the extent of a single shilling, but, still, I imagine no law can take away not merely a man's goods, but also his brains. If you can get any Vice-Chancellor to compel me to explain how to make my colours, without my assistance, of course I must bow to his decision, though, in that case, I should take leave to tell his Honour that although some colour-maker might be able to make use of the information, an accountant certainly never could."

Hearing which sentence Mr. Swanland stared. He had never before seen Mortomley roused.

He did not know each man has his weak point, and that Mortomley's pregnable spot lay close to the colours himself had begotten.

Homewood, his business, his house, his furniture, his horses, his carriages, his plant, his connection, Mortomley had yielded without a struggle, but his mental children he could not so relinquish, nor would he. Upon that point Mortomley, generally pliable, was firm, and consequently, after an amount of bickering only a degree less unpleasant to the trustee than to the bankrupt, Mortomley shook the dust of Salisbury House off his feet, declaring his intention of never entering it again.

As he passed down the staircase he met Mr. Asherill.

"Ah! Mr. Mortomley, and *how* are *you?*" cried that gentleman with effusion. "Getting on pretty well, eh? Had your discharge, of course? No. Why they ought to have given it to you long ago. So glad to see you looking so well. *Good*-bye, God bless you."

Never in his life had Mortomley felt more tempted to do anything than he did at that

moment to pitch the old hypocrite downstairs.

" My discharge !" he exclaimed, when he
was recounting the incidents of the day to his
wife, " and the vagabond knew it was never
intended I should have it. Looking well !
why, just as I was going out into the street,
Gibbons ran up against me.

" ' What's the matter, Mortomley ?' he
said, ' you look like a ghost,' and he made
me go back into the passage, and sent for some
brandy, and he hailed a cab, and remarking, ' Perhaps you have not got much money
loose about you, take this, and you can pay
me when you are next in town, six months
hence will do,' he forced his purse into my
hand. I used to think hardly of Gibbons, but
he is not a bad fellow as times go."

" You will never go to Salisbury House
again, Archie ?" she asked.

" Never, Dolly. Never, that I declare most
positively."

" Cannot we go into the country, then, for a
time ?" she suggested.

"I should like to go anywhere away from London," he answered.

After a short time she led the conversation back to his interview with Mr. Swanland.

"I cannot imagine," she said, "how it happens that amongst the papers that went from Homewood they never happened to find any of your formulæ."

"It would have puzzled them to do that," he answered, opening his tired eyes and looking at her with an expression she could not exactly understand.

"You must have had formulæ," she persisted.

"Well, yes," he agreed; "perhaps you think they extended to eight volumes of manuscript bound in morocco. You poor little woman, it would be a bad thing for colour-makers if trade secrets were not more easily carried than all that comes to. Look," and taking out his pocket-book he handed her a couple of sheets of note-paper, "every receipt of mine worth having is written down there; they are all clear enough to me, though if I lost them to-morrow they would prove Greek to any other person."

" Could you explain them to me?" she asked.

" Not now, dear," he answered, " I feel very tired; I think I could go to sleep." Which utterance proved the commencement of another relapse; but Dolly was not dismayed, on the contrary she wrote the very next day to Lang and said,

" Whenever Mr. Mortomley is well enough to leave town we shall go to a cottage I have taken in Hertfordshire. *All the special colours can now be made without difficulty.* There is a barn near the cottage which may be rented."

That was sufficient for Lang. Within a week he had got leave of absence, and was on his way back to England. He saw the barn, he measured up its size, he made out a list of the articles necessary, and received sufficient money from Mrs. Mortomley to pay for them.

He tried to get a fresh order from the firm that had wanted the new blue, but Mr. Miller shook his head.

"We have had enough of dealing with Mr. Mortomley at second-hand," he said, "when he is in a position to come to us and enter into an arrangement personally, possibly we may be able to do business." Which was just —though he did not know it—as if he had said, "When Mr. Mortomley has been to the moon and comes back again, we will resume negotiations with him."

"However, there is a trade to be done, ma'am," said Lang confidently, "and when I have finished my job, which will be in six weeks, I am thankful to say, for I am sick of the place and of those outlandish foreigners who can talk nothing but gibberish, we will do it."

"We shall have to be content with small beginnings though," suggested Mrs. Mortomley, whose views were indeed of the most modest description.

"And then at the end of a twelvemonth we shall not be ashamed to count our profits," agreed Lang, and he left assuring Dolly that his stay among the "mounseers," as he styled

all persons who had not been privileged to
first see the light in Great Britain, would be
short as he could make it.

He had set his heart upon being back in
time to attend the final sale at Homewood;
but if he was quick Mr. Swanland proved
quicker, and before his return another act in the
liquidation play was finished, and all the vats,
coppers, mills, boilers, and other paraphernalia
in which Mortomley's soul had once rejoiced
were scattered to the four winds of Heaven.

When Dolly saw the preliminary advertise-
ments announcing that the extensive and
valuable plant of a colour-maker would shortly
be offered for sale, she lowered her flag so far
as to write to Mr. Dean asking him to buy
Black Bess.

She requested this, she said, as a special
favour,—she would be more than grateful if
he could give the pretty creature a good home.
To which Mr. Dean indited a long and pompous reply. He stated that his stables only
held so many horses, that each stall had its
occupant, that he had long given up riding,

and that Black Bess would not be a match for any carriage horse of the height he habitually purchased; he remarked that she was too light even for his single brougham, and that it would be a pity to keep such an animal merely to run to and from the station in a dog-cart. Finally, Mr. Dean believed excessive affection for any dumb animal to be a mistake; Providence had given them for the use of man, and if when a horse ceased to be of service to a person in a superior rank of life, it were retained in idleness from any feeling of sentiment, what, asked Mr. Dean, would those in an inferior station do for animals? This was not very *apropos* of Black Bess—at that stage of her existence, at all events,—but it was *apropos* of the fact that Mr. Dean had the day before sold a horse which for fifteen years had served him faithfully, and got its knees cut through the carelessness of a spruce young groom,—sold this creature to which he might well have given the run of the meadows in summer and the straw-yards in winter, for six pounds.

Antonia, on whom all the traditions of Homewood had not been spent in vain, remonstrated with her husband on " the cruelty of sending the old thing away," but her words produced no effect on Mr. Dean.

" Archie Mortomley never would sell a horse that had been long about Homewood," she said.

" I dare say not, my dear," answered Mr. Dean; " but then you see it is attention to these small details that has enabled me to keep Elm Park. It was the want of that attention which drove Mr. Mortomley out of Homewood."

Upon the top of this came Mrs. Mortomley's letter. Mr. Dean devoted a whole morning to answering that letter, and then insisted upon reading his effusion aloud to his wife.

" I think I have put that very clearly," he said when he had quite finished; " I hope Mrs. Mortomley will lay what I have expressed to heart."

" If you knew anything of Mrs. Mortomley you would never send her that epistle," retorted Antonia. "She will read it to her friends, she will mimic your tone, your accent, your manner; she will borrow a pair of eyeglasses, and let them drop off her nose in the middle of each sentence; and, in a word, she will make the written wisdom of Mr. Dean of Elm Park as thoroughly ridiculous as I have often heard her make your spoken remarks."

Mr. Dean reddened, but answered with considerable presence of mind that the possession of such a wife had no doubt hastened Mortomley's ruin as much as his fatal inattention to small details.

" Perhaps so," agreed Mrs. Dean, " but still she will help him to bear being ruined with equanimity. Dolly never was dull, and, I declare, when one comes to realize how fearfully dull almost every person is, I feel as if she must, by that one virtue, have condoned all the rest of her sins."

Which was really a very hard phrase for Mr. Dean to hear proceed from the lips of the woman he had honoured so far as to make mistress of Elm Park.

But Mrs. Dean was mistaken about Dolly, and Mr. Dean need have felt no fear that ever again she would make him the butt at which to aim the shafts of ridicule. For her the champagne of mirth had ceased to sparkle; for her there was no fun in pompous respectability; for her the glittering sparkle of wit had come to be but as a flare of light to one with a maddening headache.

The cakes and ale of life had been for her, but they were for her no more. Dolly, my Dolly, you were right when you said that last look on the dead face of Homewood killed you, —for the Dolly of an earlier time, so bright, so gracious, so happy, so young-looking, as girl, as wife, as mother, you were from thenceforth never beheld by human being.

CHAPTER VI.

SAUVE QUI PEUT.

WHEN Mr. Swanland had sold off all the plant of Homewood, and got the best prices he could for Mortomley's carts and horses, Black Bess included, who had for months been so badly groomed that the auctioneer entered her as "One Brown Mare, Black Bess,"—he began to cast about him how anything more could be got out of Mortomley.

He knew he had about squeezed the orange dry, but he knew a considerable amount of juice had been lost—through "no fault of his own,"—and he consequently set his wits to work to see how that spilled liquor could be replaced.

It was not long before inspiration came to him, and when it did he summoned another meeting of the committee.

At that meeting he gravely proposed that Mortomley should be invited to bid for the remaining book debts, the books, and his discharge. The question was discussed gravely —and as gravely agreed to—though three, at all events, of the committee intended Mortomley never should have his discharge; and accordingly the same evening Mr. Swanland, who really could not dictate to a shorthand-writer, did something which passed muster for dictation, so that eventually Mortomley received a letter asking him to make an offer for the purchase of all the good things duly mentioned.

Now considering that Mortomley had been stripped as clean of all worldly belongings as the Biblical traveller who fell among thieves; considering a man in process of liquidation is in the same state as regards the inability to make personal contracts as a bankrupt; considering Dolly had not a halfpenny left of her fortune, and that friends possessed of great

wealth are not in the habit of rushing forward
at such times as these with frantic entreaties
for their purses to be made use of,—there was
a humour about this letter which might have
excited the risible muscles of a looker-on.

But there was no looker-on—there were
only the players; there were only Dolly and
Mr. Swanland in fact, and arrayed in her grey
silk skirt, in her black velvet puffings, in her
great plaits of hair, in her atom of a bonnet,
in light gloves, in the smallest of jackets, and
the largest of what then did service for *pouffs,*
Dolly went to have her quarrel out with the
trustee.

In which laudable design she was frustrated.
Mr. Swanland chanced to be at home laid up
with bronchitis, so Dolly saw instead Mr.
Asherill, and expressed to him her opinion
about the demerits of the firm.

She was not at all reticent in what she said,
and Mr. Asherill, spite of his hypocritical
manners and suave address, got the worst
of it.

He tried quoting Scripture, but Dolly outdid him there. He tried platitudes, but Dolly ridiculed both them and him. He tried conciliation, and she defied him.

" That is a dreadful woman," thought Mr. Asherill, when she finally sailed out of the office, leaving a general impression of silk, velvet, flowers, lace, feathers, and eau-de-cologne behind her. " I'll never see her again."

Poor Dolly, she must have been less or more than woman had she failed to array herself in her most gorgeous apparel when she went forth to do battle with her enemies.

There had been a latent hope in Mr. Swanland's mind that the Mortomleys either were possessed of money or knew of those who would advance it, and he felt, therefore, proportionably disappointed when Mr. Asherill assured him it was all " no good."

" She has her clothes and he has his brains if it ever please the Almighty to restore him his full faculties," summed up Mr. Asherill, "but they have nothing else; on that point you may give yourself no further trouble. Have you heard about Kleinwort?"

"Kleinwort, no! What about him?"

"He has gone."

"Gone! Where?"

"Ah! now you puzzle me. He has left England, at all events."

"And Forde?"

"I suppose we shall know more about Forde three months hence."

Was it true? Aye, indeed, it was. The little foreigner who loved his so dear Forde, the clever adventurer, sworn to see that devoted friend safe at all events,—the gross humbug, who had for years and years been cheating, not more honest, perhaps, but slower English folks, as only foreigners can, had performed as neat a dance upon horseshoes as that other celebrated foreigner who posted to Dover whilst an audience that had paid fabulous prices in expectation of seeing the performance sat in a London theatre waiting his advent.

Mr. Kleinwort was gone.

In spite of that half-yearly meeting already mentioned, where every person connected with St. Vedast Wharf made believe to be so pleased with everything, Mr. Forde found, as the weeks and months went by, that matters were becoming very difficult for him to manage— horribly difficult in fact.

His directors grew more captious and more interfering. They wanted to know a vast deal too much of the actual working of the concern. Instead of spreading out their arms any further, they were inclined to narrow the limits of their operations. They thought it was high time to put several transactions of the Company upon a more business footing, and words were dropped occasionally about their intention for the future, of placing their trade upon some more solid basis, which words filled Mr. Forde with misgiving.

Amongst other persons with whom the directors desired to curtail their dealings, was Mr. Kleinwort, and about the same period Mr. Agnew casually observed that he thought the various mining speculations in which the Company were so largely engaged, might, with advantage, be gradually and with caution closed.

He remarked that he thought such outside transactions were calculated to divert attention from their more legitimate operations, and said he considered unless the capital of the Company could be largely increased, it would be more prudent, in the then state of the money-market and general want of confidence in the public in limited companies, to confine themselves to a different, if apparently less remunerative, class of business. Of these words of wisdom Mr. Forde spoke scoffingly to Mr. Kleinwort, but they made him uneasy nevertheless; and he proposed to Kleinwort that he and Werner and the German should take Mortomley's works, the lease of which— it was after the sale of plant at Homewood— could be had for a nominal price, so that they might have something to fall back on, in case the directors at St. Vedast Wharf should at any time take it into their heads to close transactions with Mr. Kleinwort, and, as a natural consequence, to dismiss Mr. Forde.

"They are ungrateful enough for anything," finished the manager, and to this Kleinwort agreed.

"They have hearts as the nether millstone," he said, " and, what is worse, their brains are all soft, addled ; but still we will not take the colour-works yet. I have one plan, but the pear is not ripe quite. When it is, you will know, and then you shall exclaim—' Oh ! what a clever little fellow is that Kleinwort of mine.'"

Whatever opinions Mr. Forde might entertain about Mr. Kleinwort's cleverness, his directors were becoming somewhat doubtful concerning his solvency.

" He is expecting a bill from a correspondent of his in Germany for a large amount in a few days, and he has promised to let me have it," explained Mr. Forde, and then, after his tormentors left him free, he sent round to Mr. Kleinwort, saying, " You *must* let me have that foreign bill without delay," to which Kleinwort turning down a piece of the paper, wrote "To-morrow," and putting the manager's note in a fresh envelope returned it to him.

In fault of any better security then obtainable, this bill would next day have been placed to Mr. Kleinwort's credit on the books of the firm, had Mr. Agnew not chanced to take it in his hand. After looking at it for a moment, his eye fell on the date of the stamp, and he at once wrote a few words on a scrap of paper and pushed the memorandum and the acceptance over to the chairman.

"Had not we better request Mr. Kleinwort to attend and explain," he asked.

To which the chairman agreeing, Mr. Forde, who had left the board-room for a moment, and now reappeared, was asked to send to Mr. Kleinwort and say the directors would be glad if he could come round for a few minutes.

"There is something wrong about that acceptance," wrote the manager in pencil. "For God's sake think what it can be, and show yourself at once."

Round came the German to show himself. He entered the board-room wiping his forehead, and after smiling and bowing, said,

"You did wish to see me, gentlemen," and he stole a quick look at the faces turned to his.

"Yes, about this bill," suggested Mr. Agnew. "May I inquire on what date you sent it to Germany?"

"I never sent that bill to Germany at all," answered Kleinwort. "I did send one, his fellow, ten days' back, but he have not returned; he will not now. My good friend and correspondent turned up last night at mine house from Denmark, where he had business, and he gave me his signature not ten minutes before it was despatched to this your place."

Hearing which the chairman nodded to Mr. Agnew, and said, "That explains the matter," adding, "thank you, Mr. Kleinwort; we are very sorry to have given you so much trouble."

"No, no, no, not trouble, by no means," declared the German vehemently, and he passed out of the board-room and left the wharf as he had entered it, wiping the perspiration off his forehead.

"Pouf!" he exclaimed, as he re-entered his office, and after pulling off his coat poured out half-a-tumbler of neat brandy, and swallowed it at a draught. " There has been too much of this, Kleinwort, my dear fellow, a few straws more would break even thy camel's back."

During the remainder of that day Mr. Kleinwort was too busy to spare more than a minute even to Mr. Forde, when that gentleman called to see him. The next morning he was too ill to come to business, and Mr. Forde, who felt anxious naturally concerning the health of a man, bound to stand by him through all chances and changes, went up to his house to ascertain what was the matter.

" I must get away for a week," declared the invalid, who looked ill enough to have warranted his saying he must get away for three months. " It has all been too much for me. A few days' quiet, and the sea, and the shells, and the bright ships sailing by, and I come back better than well. I go on Monday to Hastings, and you must so manage as to come to spend Saturday and Sunday in that peace so profound. Promise that it be we see you."

In perfect good faith Mr. Forde did promise that Kleinwort should be gratified thus far, but

it was not in his nature to let a man go away
from town and fail to remind him by means of
every night's post about the trouble and
anxiety he had left behind him. To these
communications the manager received no reply
whatever until the fourth day, when having
despatched a more pressing and irritable note
than usual there arrived this telegram.

"Monday will not be long. All suspense
for you then over. Till then torment not me
with business. We expect you for Saturday."

But it so happened that when Saturday
came Mr. Forde found himself unable to leave
London, and was compelled to telegraph apolo-
gies and regrets to his friend.

He waited at the wharf for an hour after
the clerks left, expecting a reply to this communication, but at the end of that time wended
his way home, thinking that most probably
Mr. Kleinwort would address his answer there.
Night closed, however, and no telegram arrived.

"He was out, no doubt," considered Mr.
Forde, "and, as he is to be in London so soon,
did not think it worth while to send a message

till his return;" and with these comforting re-
flections, and the still more comforting fact of
Monday, which was to end all suspense, being
close at hand, Mr. Forde went to bed and
slept soundly.

Monday came, and Mr. Forde was at Mr.
Kleinwort's office so early that the head clerk
was just turning the key in the lock as he
reached the landing.

"Mr. Kleinwort come yet?" asked Mr.
Forde.

"I have not seen him, sir. I should scarcely
think he could be here yet."

"Any letter from him?" asked the manager,
entering the office, and taking the letters out of
the clerk's unresisting hands he looked at each
superscription curiously.

"I will look round again shortly," he remarked, after he had examined the correspondence once more, and felt in the letter-box to
make sure no missive had been overlooked.

"Very well, sir," said Mr. Kleinwort's
clerk.

The day wore on, and Mr. Forde looked

"round again" often, but still with the same result. He telegraphed to Hastings, but elicited no reply. By the evening's post he wrote requesting that a telegram might be sent to the wharf immediately on receipt of his letter to say by which train Mr. Kleinwort might be expected in town.

He received no telegram; nothing had been heard from Mr. Kleinwort at that gentleman's office; the head clerk feared he could not be so well; and Mr. Forde started off by the next train to Hastings.

Arrived there, he ascertained Mr. and Mrs. Kleinwort had left for London on the previous Friday evening.

By the time Mr. Forde again reached the City all business was over for the day, and the offices closed for the night, therefore the unhappy manager, dreading he knew not what, fearing some evil to which he felt afraid to give a shape or a name, repaired to Mr. Kleinwort's private residence.

He looked up at the house, and as he did so his heart sank within him; not a light was to

be seen in any one of the windows, the lower
shutters were closed, there was straw littering
about the garden. His worst enemy might
have pitied him as he stood there hoping he
was dreaming, hoping he should wake to find
that he had been struggling with some horrible
nightmare.

When he could gather strength to do it, he
began knocking at the door—knocking till he
woke the deserted house with echoes that
simulated the sound of hurrying feet—knocking till the neighbours opened their doors, and
put their heads out of the windows to ascertain what was the matter.

"There is no one in that house, sir," shouted
an irascible gentleman from the next balcony.

"There is no use in your trying to knock
the door down. The house is empty, sir. The
family left a week ago, and the last of the
furniture was removed on Saturday."

"Where have they gone?" asked Mr.
Forde in a weak husky voice, which sounded
to his own ears like that of some different
person.

"To South America. Mr. Kleinwort has got an appointment there under his own government."

That was enough. The manager knew for certain Kleinwort had thrown him over, that he had eight days' start of any one who might try to follow.

How it had been managed; how the Hastings juggle was performed; who had helped him to hoodwink those who might be interested concerning his whereabouts, he felt too sick and dizzy even to imagine.

There was only a single fact he was able to realise; namely, that between him and ruin there stood now but one man, and that man Henry Werner.

CHAPTER VII.

MORTOMLEY UNDERSTANDS AT LAST.

THE summer following that autumn and winter when Mortomley's Estate was in full course of liquidation proved, if not the hottest ever remembered, at least sufficiently warm to render Londoners who had to remain in town extremely impatient of their captivity, and to induce all those who could get away to make a rush for any place within a reasonable distance where sea-breezes or fresh air could be obtained.

It was a summer in which everything was as dull as can well be imagined. Trade was dreadful; each man seemed losing money, and no man confessed to a balance of five pounds

at his bankers'. If City people were to be
believed, a series of unprecedented misfortunes
compelled them, one and all, to ask for outstanding accounts and to request the return of
such small amounts of money as in moments
of mental aberration they had been induced to
lend to their impecunious friends, whilst it
happened most unfortunately that a series of
disappointments and misfortunes equally unprecedented prevented the payment of accounts and the return of loans.

Making, however, due allowance for excuses
and exaggeration, things were very bad
indeed. That badness affected all trades—
touched all ranks. People were not rich
enough to be ill, they could not afford to die,
and so even the doctors and the undertakers
found things hard, and believed fees and
feathers had gone out of fashion.

" Persons in course of liquidation were to
be envied," so Mr. Swanland with a faint at-
tempt at humour assured his visitors, while
Mr. Asherill declared that really he wished he
could go into the ' Gazette ' and so get a holi-
day.

If you were on sufficiently intimate terms
to inquire concerning the fruitful vine and the
olive branches belonging to any City man, you
were certain to hear the vine and the olives
had been transplanted temporarily to some
easily accessible resting-place, to which the
husband and father declared to you upon his
word of honour he had not the means of proceeding on that especial Saturday afternoon
when you spoke to him in Finch Lane.

Nevertheless, had your way been his, you
would have met him an hour after, taking his
ticket for some well-known terminus.

Even Mr. Dean could not manage to leave
town, and Mrs. Dean was, therefore, at Scar-
borough with some Essex friends who had
invited her to join their party.

Mrs. Werner was at Dassell with her children. The old lord was dead, and that
Charley, who had once wished to marry his
cousin, proposed taking up his residence at the
family seat. If this resolution were carried
out, Mrs. Trebasson intended to leave the hall,
notwithstanding her nephew's cordially ex-

pressed hope that she would still consider it her home.

Naturally, therefore, Mrs. Werner availed herself of the opportunity, still left of paying a long visit to the old place, and Mr. Werner had begged her not to hurry back, as " he could do very well without her " — which utterance he did not intend to be ungracious, neither did his wife so understand it.

As for Mortomley and his wife, they were far away from London.

In one of the most remote parts of Hertfordshire where woods cover the lonely country for miles, where the silvery Lea flows through green fields on its way to the sea, never dreaming of the horror and filth it will have to encounter ere mingling with the Thames— where the dells are in the sweet spring time carpeted with violets, blue and white, that load the air with perfume—where rabbits scud away through copses starred with primroses— where jays plume their brilliant feathers in the golden sunshine—where squirrels look with bright curious eyes at the solitary passer-

by—where pheasants scarcely move out of the
way of a stranger's footsteps—where, save for
the singing of birds, and the humming of in-
sects, and the bleating of sheep, there is a
silence that can be felt—Dolly had found a
home.

As seen from the road as picturesque a
cottage as painter need have desired to see,
but only a poor scrap of a cottage architectu-
rally considered—a labourer's cottage origi-
nally, and yet truly as Dolly described it to
Mrs. Werner—a very pretty little place.

The ground on which it stood rose suddenly
from the road, and the tiny garden in front
sloped down to the highway at a sharp angle.
On one side was a large orchard, which went
with the house, and on the other a great field
of growing wheat already turning colour.

Behind the cottage was first its own ample
vegetable garden, and then one of the woods
I have mentioned, which formed a background
for the red-tiled roof and tumbledown chim-
neys of the Mortomleys' new home.

Dolly had seen the advertisement of a place

she thought might suit to let in this locality,
and so chanced to penetrate into wilds so far
from London.

As usual, the place advertised was in every
respect undesirable, and Dolly wore herself out
wandering about interminable lanes looking
for a vacant cottage and finding none.

All this was in the early spring when the
leaves were only putting forth, when Daffodils,
Mezerion, and American currant alone decked
the modest flower-gardens—when nature, in a
word, had not yet decked herself in the beautiful garments of May, or in the glorious
apparel of the year's maturer age.

But Dolly knew how that pleasant country
place would look when the hawthorn was in
bloom, and the roses climbing over the rustic
porches, and the corn cut and standing in
goodly sheaves under the summer sun.

There was not a mood or tense of country
life Dolly did not understand and love, and
she felt like a child disappointed of a new
toy while wending her way back to the station
to think her search had proved all in vain.

She was in this mood as she drew near the cottage I have described.

"I could be quite satisfied even with that," she considered. "I could soon make it look different;" and she stood leaning over the gate and picturing the place with grass close under the window, with a few evergreens planted against the palings, with a rustic garden-chair with rustic baskets filled with flowers, on the scrap of lawn herself had imagined.

As she so stood an old woman came to the door and looked down the walk at the stranger curiously.

"I was admiring your dear little place," said Dolly apologetically. "I think it is so sweet and quiet."

The woman trotted down to the gate on hearing these words of praise, and answered,

"Aye, it is main pretty in the summer, when the flowers are in full blow, and the trees in full leaf. I tell my master we shall often think of it in the strange land we are going to."

Now this sentence perplexed Dolly; owing to

the tone in which it was spoken, she could not tell whether the woman meant she and her husband were going to heaven or to foreign parts, so she asked no question.

She only said, " I am sure you will think it no trouble to give me a glass of water. I have been walking a long way, and I am very tired."

" Come in and rest yourself then," the old lady exclaimed heartily, and she conducted Dolly indoors, and dusted a chair for her, and brought her the water ice-cold ; and having elicited that Mrs. Mortomley had come all the way from London, that she had walked miles, that she had been to look at Hughes's house, and that neither bite nor sup had passed her lips since breakfast save that glass of cold water, she asked if her visitor would not like a cup of tea. The kettle was on, she said, and she could mash the tea in a few minutes.

Dolly was delighted, she wanted the tea, and she rejoiced in the adventure. What though the bread was home-made bread and as heavy as lead, to quote poor Hood ; what though the tea was "mashed" till it was black in the face; what though the sugar was brown and of a treacley consistence,—the guest brought to the repast an appetite which charmed her hostess and amazed herself.

While Dolly sipped her tea, for she understood the teapot had no great force of resistance and could not hold out to great extremity, and the "darling old lady," as Mrs. Mortomley called her for ever afterwards, drank hers out of a saucer, the two women got into a friendly conversation, and the elder told the younger how she and her master were going to America to their only son, who, after being "awful wild," and a "fearful radical," often going well-nigh to break his father's heart, who had set "great store" by his boy, had started off fifteen years previously "for Ameriky unbeknown to living soul."

Arrived there it was the old story of the prodigal repeated, with a difference.

At home he had wasted his substance and neglected his parents. Abroad he repented him of his evil doings, and worked as hard in a strange country as he had idled in England.

He had married well, and was a rich man, and all he desired now was that his father and mother should make their home near him, share his prosperity, and see their grand-children.

"And so, ma'am, we are going as soon as ever we can let the house and sell our bits of furniture. The house we could get rid of fast enough, but no one wants the furniture, and my husband he is loth to let it go for what the brokers offer."

"What do they offer?" asked Dolly.

"For every stick and stool in the house thirty shillings."

"And how much do you think they ought to give?" asked Dolly.

"Why my master he says as how we ought not to take less nor five pound for the furniture, and two pound for the cropped garden and fowl-house, and sty and woodshed, all of which he builded with his own hands; but there's a sight of counting in that money, and

people like us have all their beds and chairs
and tables, and I wish he'd take the dealer's
offer and be done with it, for I am longing to
see my boy once more."

Dolly turned her face aside, and looked at
the fire.

"What is the rent of this place?" she inquired.

"Four pound eleven a year, ma'am; and
though that do sound high, still it is a cheap
place at the money, for there's a fine big
garden and that orchard you see, and it
needn't stand empty an hour if only my
master would give in about the furniture."

"How many rooms have you?" Dolly asked.

"We have as good as four upstair; but
two of them are open like on the stairs. We
use them for storing things, and there is this
house; we call the front room 'the house' in
these parts, ma'am, and the back place, and
another back place where the stairs lead out,
and—"

"Might I see it?" Dolly entreated, "I
should like to see it so much."

"You'll excuse the place being in a bit of a muddle?" answered the other, as she led the way about her small territory.

"Good Heavens! if this is a muddle, what must apple-pie order be?" thought Mrs. Mortomley, as she looked at the well-scrubbed stairs, at the snow-white boards, at the chest of drawers bees-waxed till she saw her own reflection in them better than in the looking-glass, off which half the quicksilver had peeled; at the patch-work counterpane, which, though probably half a century old, still shone forth resplendent with red and yellow and green, and all the colours of the rainbow.

"I do not care to see the garden," said Dolly when they were once more in the back place; "and I have seen the orchard. I will take the house off your hands, and your furniture, and your crops, at your own price; I have not so much money with me, but I will leave you what I have in my purse, and I will send down again any day you name, in order to pay you the balance still owing and to take possession."

"You, ma'am!" repeated the woman.

"Yes," answered Dolly; "I have a husband who is in bad health, and I must get him away from London for a short time. We cannot afford to take a large house. We can make this answer our purpose, so now give me a receipt for three pounds ten, on account—and—"

"I can't write," was the reply.

"Well, I will leave my address, and your husband can send me one," suggested Dolly.

"He is no more a schollard nor me," said the woman.

Was this the reason Dolly wondered, why at their age they were willing to give up their home and country and go so far away to join the whilom prodigal? Not to be able to send a line, without that line being indited by other fingers, seen by other eyes; not to be able to understand the contents of a letter save by the aid of a third person's reading! it was certainly very pitiful, Dolly considered.

"It is of no consequence," she remarked, after a moment's pause devoted to thinking this aspect of the educational question over. "Here are three pounds ten shillings, and perhaps you can get some of your neighbours to send me a line, saying when you wish to leave. Good-bye, I hope you may have a pleasant voyage, and find your son well and happy at the end of it."

And so Dolly retired mistress of the position ; and so all unconsciously she had frustrated the schemes of the poor old father, who, not wishing to cross his wife, and not wanting to leave England, had put what he considered a prohibitory price on his effects, and refused to leave unless that were given for them.

"It is God's will, and I dare not gainsay it," he muttered to himself, when he grasped the full meaning of his wife's breathless revelation. "But it is nought less nor a miracle —what parson tells us a Sundays ain't a bit more wonderful. It is main hard though, for me at my age though, to be taken at my word like this."

From which utterance it will be seen he never thought of going back from his word ;

indeed, regarding Dolly's visit as he did,
it is probable he imagined some judgment
might fall upon him if he tried to put any
further impediment in the way.

As for Dolly, once she got possession of the
place, she sent Esther down with full directions
how she was to proceed to make it habit-
able. Papers were forwarded from London—
papers cheap, light, pretty ; and with the help
of two local workmen, who " contracted " for
the job, the whole house was whitewashed,
papered, and painted, in ten days. Dogs took
the place of the old-fashioned rickety grate, the
outer door was taken off its hinges, and a new
one, the upper part of which was of glass, put
in its place. A modest porch of trellis-work
shaded this door, and over it grew roses and
honeysuckle, which were duly trained by a
superannuated labourer, who, thankful for a
week's work, laid down that grass-plot Dolly's
heart desired, at a rate of wage which made
Mrs. Mortomley feel ashamed as she paid him
the price agreed on.

To persons who have been accustomed to

yield up their houses to a professional deco-
rator, and allow him to work his will as to
cost of material and price of labour, and the
amount of improvement to be effected, it may
seem that Mrs. Mortomley must, in making her
old cottage into a new one, have spent a considerable sum of money.

This was not the case ; and yet when Dolly
came to go through her accounts, which
meant, in her case, counting over the sovereigns still remaining, she felt she had exceeded
the original estimate it was her intention to ad-
here to, and that she must economize very
strictly in the future if her noble was not soon
to be brought down to ninepence.

Mr. Mortomley had with much difficulty ex-
tracted ten pounds from the treasury at
Salisbury House, for his attendance at Mr.
Swanland's offices, and a wonderful thing had
happened to Dolly.

Rupert not merely repaid the money he
borrowed, but added twenty pounds to the
amount.

"I have had a great piece of good fortune

happen to me," he wrote, "and I send you share of it; I leave for the Continent next month, in company with Mr. Althorpe, a young gentleman possessed of plenty of money and no brains to speak of. He pays all my expenses, and gives me a handsome salary in addition. You may expect to see me next Saturday. I long to see your cottage, and will arrange to stay until Tuesday morning."

So Rupert was the first visitor, recalling the old days departed, who crossed the threshold of the new home, and to whom Dolly could expatiate on the improvements she had effected.

"You have done wonders," said Rupert, standing beside her in the little garden which commanded a view of the Lee, winding away through pleasant meadows. "It is really a marvellous little nest to have constructed out of your materials, but," he added suddenly, "Archie does not like it—Archie is breaking his heart here."

"Archie will have to like it," returned Dolly, and there was a tone in her voice

Rupert had never heard in it before. "There is no good in a man kicking against the pricks, and pining for things even those who love him best cannot give him. I shall have to tell him, Rupert; I feel that, whether ill or well, it is time he took his share of the burden with me. The sooner he knows, the sooner he will be able to look our position straight in the face. I wish I was not such a coward. I cannot endure the idea of letting him into the secret that everything has gone, that there is not a thing left."

She spoke less passionately than despairingly. In truth, the change from which she had anticipated such good results, proved the last straw which broke her back.

She, understanding their position, had felt thankful to realise that even so humble a home was possible for them until her husband's health should be re-established, and the sight of his ill-concealed despair when he beheld the cottage, proved a shock as great to her as his new home to Mortomley.

For months and months she had been reconciling herself to the inevitable—schooling herself to forget the past and look forward to a future when Archie would take an interest in the modest little factory she and Lang were to prepare, and learn to find happiness in the tiny home she had tried so hard to beautify— but it came upon him suddenly. He had not realised the full change in his circumstances when he left Homewood, or when he struggled back to consciousness from long illness at Upper Clapton; not when he had to attend at Mr. Swanland's offices; not when the Thames Street warehouse was closed, and one of his own clerks started a feeble business there on the strength of his late employer's name and connection; not when the last sale took place at Homewood—no, not once till on the morning after his arrival at Wood Cottage, (so Dolly christened the new home), he rose early, and walking round the house and surveying his small territory, comprehended vaguely there was something still for him to know; that Dolly was keeping some terrible secret.

" He knows all about it as well as you, you may depend," Rupert said in reply to Dolly's last sentence ; " nothing you can tell him now will be news to him."

But Dolly shook her head.

Her instinct was clearer than Rupert's reason, and she felt certain if her husband only knew the worst, he would nerve himself to face it more bravely than he could this vague intangible trouble.

" I will tell him," she declared to Rupert, and then like a coward put off doing so till Mortomley himself broke the ice by asking,

" Dolly, how long do you propose remaining in this charming locality ?"

" Do you not think it charming ?" she inquired. " I think the walks about are lovely, and the air so pure, and the scenery so calm and peaceful—"

" Granted, my love ; but it is a place one would soon grow very tired of. I must honestly confess I find time hang very heavily on my hands already."

"Don't say that, don't," she entreated.

"But, Dolly, if it be true why should I not say it?" he inquired.

"Because, my poor dear," and Dolly laid a trembling hand on his shoulder, "I am afraid you will have to stay here and learn to like and find your interests in it."

He took her hand in his, and turned so that he could see her face.

"What is it, dear, you are keeping from me? Is there any difficulty about getting the interest of your money. Mr. Daniells is in London I know, and the matter now ought to be put right. Tell me all about it, dear—why are we in this place, and why do you say we must remain here?"

"Because," Dolly began, and then stopped, hesitating how to frame her sentence.

"Because what?" he asked a little impatiently. "Come, dear, out with it; the trouble will not seem half so great or insurmountable when you share it with me. Because—"

"Because I have no money, Archie, now,

except just a very, very little; because that has gone like everything else."

"Do you mean your fortune?" he asked.

"Yes, dear, the whole of it," she answered, determined he should know the worst at last.

"My God!" said Mortomley, and the expression sounded strange, coming from the lips of a man who rarely gave vent to any vehemence of feeling. "What a fool I have been! what a wicked, short-sighted, senseless fool! why don't you speak hardly to me, Dolly—I who have ruined you and Lenore?"

She stooped down and kissed him.

"Archie, I don't care a straw about the money; I did at first, and I was afraid, but I am not afraid now; if only you will be content and brave, and ready to believe small beginnings sometimes make great endings."

But he made no reply. He only rose, and walking to the door flung it open, and stood looking out over the pleasant landscape.

Dolly feigned not to notice him. She went to her work-table and began turning over her tapes and cottons with restless fingers, waiting, waiting for her husband to speak.

Then in a moment there came a tremendous crash, and Mortomley was lying on the matting which covered the floor, like one dead.

CHAPTER VIII.

MR. WERNER ASKS A FAVOUR.

ABOUT the very happiest hour of Dolly Mortomley's life was one in which her husband, still weak and languid, after watching her gliding about his sick-room, said—feebly it is true, but still as his wife had not heard him speak since the time of his first attack at Homewood—"My poor Dolly."

It was the voice of the olden time—of the never-to-be-forgotten past, when if she made burdens he was strong enough to carry them. In that pleasant country place the cloud which had for so long a time obscured his mental vision, was rent asunder, and the man's faculties

that had so long lain dormant, were given back
to him once more.

Dolly was right.   No one save herself knew
how ill Mortomley had been during all that
weary time at Homewood, during the long
sickness at Clapton, during all the months
which followed when superficial observers
deemed him well.

Though on that bright summer's morning,
with his haggard face turned towards the
sunlight, he looked more like a man ready for
his coffin than fit to engage once more in the
battle of life, there was a future possible for
Mortomley again—possible even in those remote wilds where newspapers never came, except by post, and then irregularly ; where the
rector called upon them once a week at least ;
where the rector's wife visited Dolly every
day during the worst part of her husband's
illness ; where fruit and flowers came every
day from the Great House of the neighbourhood by direction of the owner, who was
rarely resident ; and where the gentry who
were resident thought it not beneath their

dignity to leave cards for the poor little woman who was in such sore affliction, and who would have been so lonely without the kindly sympathy of those who had—seeing her at church—considered her style of dress most unsuitable, perfectly unaware that Dolly was wearing out the silks and satins and laces and feathers of a happier time with intentions of the truest economy

But Dolly was no longer unhappy.

"I am so thankful," she said to the rector's wife that day; "my husband is dreadfully weak still, I know, but he will get better—I feel it—I—"

But there she stopped; she could not tell any one of the old sweet memories those three words, "My poor Dolly," brought back to her mind; she could not explain how when she heard them spoken she understood Archie, her Archie, had been for a long time away, and was now come back and lying feeble it is true, but still on the highway to health in that upstairs chamber which her love had made so pretty for him.

Thus the scales of happiness vibrate, up to-day for one, down to-morrow for another.

It had been the turn of Messrs. Forde and Kleinwort once to stand between Dolly and the sunshine; it was the turn of both now to stand aside while the Mortomleys basked in it; from that very morning when Archie came back to life and reason, Mr. Forde knew for certain Kleinwort's little game was played out and that he had left England, himself not much the better for all his playing at pitch-and-toss with fortune, and every man he had ever been connected with the poorer and the sadder, and the more desperate, for his acquaintance.

Just a week after that day Dolly sat in "the house," as she still continued to call the front room, all alone.

She held work in her hand, but she was not sewing, she had a song in her heart, but she was not singing it audibly. She was very happy, and though she had cause for anxiety best known to herself, hers was not a nature to dwell upon the dark side of a picture so long as there was a bright one to it.

Upstairs Mortomley lay asleep, the soft pure air fanning his temples, and the songs of birds and the perfume of flowers influencing and colouring the matter of his dreams.

Lenore was at the Rectory spending the day. Esther had gone to the nearest town to make some purchases, and Mrs. Mortomley sat all alone.

Along the road, through the gate, up the narrow walk, came a visitor. He never looked to right or left, he never paused or hesitated for a moment, but strode straight to the door and knocked.

The door opened into "the house," which was indeed the only sitting-room the Mortomleys boasted, and Dolly rising, advanced to give him admittance. Through the glass she saw him and he saw her. For a second she hesitated, and then opening the door said, with no tone of welcome in her voice,

"Mr. Werner."

"Yes, Mrs. Mortomley, it is I," he answered. "May I come in?"

"You can come in if you like. As a matter

of taste, I should not have thought you would like—"

"As a matter of taste, perhaps not," was the reply. "As a matter of necessity, I must."

After he entered they remained standing. Mrs. Mortomley would not ask him to sit down, and for a moment his glance wandered over the room with its floor paved with white bricks, shining and bright like marble, over the centre of which was spread some India matting.

He took in the whole interior with that rapidity of perception which was natural to him. He noticed the great ferns and bright flowers piled up in the fireplace. He saw wonderful palms and distorted cacti, all presents given to Dolly, the pots hidden away in moss, which gave so oriental a character to the quaint and modest home.

He beheld the poor furniture made graceful and pretty by Dolly's taste and skill, and in the foreground of the picture he saw Mrs. Mortomley, a mere shadow of the Mrs. Mortomley he remembered, it is true, clad in a gorgeous muslin which had seen service at Homewood, her hair done up over frizzetts which seemed trying to reach to the seventh heaven, her frills as ample and her skirts as much puffed as though she was living in a Belgravian mansion.

There was no pathos of poverty about Dolly. To look at her no human being could have conceived she had passed through such an ordeal as that I have endeavoured to describe.

Somehow one does associate sadly-made dresses and hair gathered up in a small knob at the back of the head with adversity, and well as Mr. Werner knew Dolly her appearance astonished him.

"How is your husband?" he inquired at last.

"I cannot at all see why you should inquire," she replied, "but as you have inquired I am happy to say he is better, that I believe he will get well now, well and strong and capable."

"What is he doing now ?"

"He is asleep, or was ten minutes ago."

"I did not mean that, I meant in the way of business."

"I decline to answer any questions relating to our private affairs," said Dolly defiantly.

Mr. Werner merely smiled in comment, a sad smile, full of some meaning which Dolly could not fathom.

" May I sit down ?" he asked after a moment's pause.

"Certainly, though I should not have ima-gined you would care to sit down in my husband's house."

"If I had not known Mrs. Mortomley to be an exceptional woman, I should not have entered her husband's house at all."

" Mrs. Mortomley is so exceptional a woman that she desires no compliments from Mr. Werner," was the reply.

He smiled again and said,

" And I in good faith am in no mood to pay compliments to any one—not even to you, whom I want to do me a favour."

"Recalling the past, I cannot help remarking that diffidence does not appear to be one of your strongest characteristics."

"Recalling the past, you will do me this kindness for the sake of my wife."

Dolly did not answer. She wanted to understand what this favour might be before she committed herself.

"I cannot sit," he said, "unless you are seated also, and I am tired mentally and bodily. I assure you when I have told you all I have come to tell, you will not regret having extended to me courtesy as well as attention."

He placed a chair for her, and then took one himself.

"I have come to speak to you about a very serious matter—" he began.

"If it is anything concerning Archie do not go on," she interrupted entreatingly. "I have been so happy this morning, and I cannot bear to hear ill news now—I cannot!" she repeated passionately.

"Strange as it may appear to you," he said calmly, "there are other persons in England than Mr. and Mrs. Mortomley. It is a singular fact, but true nevertheless, that they are only two souls out of a population of thirty millions. I am bringing no bad news to you about your husband or his affairs; my news is bad for Leonora."

"But she is not ill," said Dolly quickly, "for I had a letter from her this morning."

"No; she is quite well, and the children are well, and I am well. There is an exhaustive budget of the state of the family health. But still what I have to say does effect Leonora. You remember your friend, Kleinwort, Mrs. Mortomley ? "

"I once saw a detestable little German called Kleinwort," she said.

"And you remember his—so dear— Forde ? "

"I remember him also."

"Well, a week ago that so dear Forde found that his devoted friend, under a pretence of ill-health and paying a visit to Hastings, had taken French leave of this country and got ten days' start of any one who might feel inclined to follow. He was not able to secure much booty in his retreat; but I fancy, all told, he has taken seven or eight thousand pounds with him, and he has let the General Chemical Company in for an amount which seems simply fabulous.

" So far Kleinwort, now for myself. A few years ago no man in London need have desired to be in a better position than that I occupied. I was healthy, wealthy, and, as I thought, wise ; I was doing a safe trade, I had a good connection ; I was as honest as City people have any right to be, and— But why do I talk of this ? I am not reciting my own biography.

" Well, the crash of 1866 came. In that crash most people lost a pot of money. Richard Halling did (and your husband's estate has since suffered for it), and I did also. If I had stopped then I could not have paid a shilling in the pound ; but no one knew this, my credit was good and my business capacity highly esteemed. So I went on, and tried my best to regain the standing I alone knew I had lost."

A carafe of water stood on a table close to where he sat. He poured out a glass and drank eagerly ere he proceeded.

"Not to weary you with details, in an evil hour my path crossed that of Forde. He wanted to build up the standing of the General Chemical Company; I wanted to ensure the stability of my own.

"Mutually we lied to each other; mutually we deceived each other. I thought him a capable scoundrel; he thought me a grasping millionaire. The day came when I understood thoroughly he had no genius whatever, even for blackguardism, but was simply a man to whom his situation was so important that he would have sacrificed his first-born to retain his post; a man who would have been honest enough had no temptation been presented to him; a man who was not possessed of sufficient moral courage to be either a saint or a sinner, who was always halting between two opinions, and whilst treading the flowery paths leading to perdition, cast regretful glances back to the dusty roads and stony highways traversed by successful virtue, whilst I—"

He paused and then went on.

" Ever since 1866 I have been a mere adventurer, building up my credit upon one
rotten foundation after another, believing
foolishly it may be and yet sincerely the turn
would come some day, and that I should
eventually be able to retrieve all—pay all."

" And I still believe," he proceeded after
a moment's pause, " that I could have got out
safe, had Swanland, for the sake of advertising
himself, not advertised your husband's failure.
Had I been able to carry out my plans, the
General Chemical Company and I had parted
company months ago. I reckoned on being
able to bribe Forde to help me to do this. He
rose to the bait, but he had not power to fulfil
his part of the bargain. There was an an-
tagonistic influence at work, and we never
traced it to its source until a few days since.
Then we found that a new director had been
quietly looking into your affair, and as a natural
consequence into the affairs of other customers.
He discovered how bills had been manipulated
and accounts cooked, how one security had

been made to do duty for six, and much more
to the same effect. It was all clumsy botched
work, but either it had really deceived the other
directors or they pretended it had, which comes
to about the same thing. However, to cut the
story short, Kleinwort, who foresaw the turn
affairs would take, has gone, and I, who did
not foresee, must go also."

" Go where ? " Dolly inquired.

" I am uncertain," he answered ; " but it is
useless my remaining to face the consequences
of my own acts."

" But do you mean to say," asked Mrs.
Mortomley, " that you intend to go away and
never return to England ? "

" That is precisely my meaning."

" And what will Leonora say ? "

" She will be very much shocked at first,
I do not doubt," was the reply ; " but
eventually, I hope, she will understand I took
the best course possible under the circumstances, and that brings me to the favour I
want you to do me. I want you to take charge
of this parcel, and give it to my wife at the end

of six months. Give it to her when she is alone, and do not mention in the meantime to any one that you have seen me, or that a packet from me is in your possession. You understand what I mean ? "

" I think so," said Dolly. " There is money in the packet, and—"

" You are shrewder than I thought," he remarked. " There is money in that parcel. You understand now why I ask you to take charge of it ? Have you any objection to do so ? "

" None whatever," was the quick reply.

" And if questions are asked ? "

" I know nothing," she answered.

" You will be silent to Leonora ? "

" Yes. I understand what you want, and I will do it. Tell me one thing, however. Some day Leonora will join you ? "

" I have faith that it is not impossible," he said, rising as he spoke. " Good-bye, Mrs. Mortomley. God bless you." And without thought he put out his hand.

Then Dolly drew back, flushing crimson. " I

do this for your wife, Mr. Werner," she said, "not for you. I cannot forget."

"You can forgive though, I hope," he pleaded. "Mrs. Mortomley, I wish before we part you would say, 'I forgive you, and I hope God will.' It is not a long sentence."

"It is a hard one," she answered; "so hard that I cannot say it."

"For my wife's sake?"

"One cannot forgive for the sake of a third person, however dear."

"Do you remember how you wished, or said you should wish, but for her, that I might be beggared and ruined—beggared more completely, ruined more utterly than you had been? The words have never died out of my memory."

"Did I say so?" Dolly asked, a little shocked, as people are sometimes apt to be, at the sound of their own hot words repeated in cold blood. "I have no doubt," she went on, "that I meant every syllable at the time, but I ought not to have meant it—I am sure I should not wish my worst enemy to pass through all we have been compelled to endure."

"In that case it will be the easier for you to shake hands and say we part friends."

"I cannot do what you ask," she said. "I might forgive had the injury been to me alone; but I cannot forget all you said about my husband, who would not have turned a dog from his door, let alone a man he had known for years. And you never wrote through all the weary months that followed to say you were sorry—you never came or sent to know whether he was living or dead—whether we were starving or had plenty. I can say with all my heart, I hope you will never through your own experience know what we suffered; but I cannot say we part friends. I cannot say I shall ever feel as a friend towards you?"

"I think you will, nevertheless, Mrs. Mortomley," he said quietly. "I think if you knew all I have suffered recently, all I was suffering when Leonora told me that night you were in the house, you would not be so hard on me now; but I cannot argue the matter with a woman who has fought her husband's battle so bravely and so persistently. There was a time when I did not like you, when I thought your husband had made a mistake in marrying you, when I regarded my wife's affection for you as an infatuation, and would have stopped the intimacy had it been possible; but I tell you now I find myself utterly in error. Regarding life from my present standpoint, I think Archie Mortomley richer in being your husband than I should consider him had he a fine business or thousands lying idle at his bankers. One can but be happy. Looking back, I believe I may honestly say since I came to man's estate, I have never known a day's true happiness."

"It is to come," she said eagerly; "there are, there must be years of happiness in store for you and Lenny."

"I do not think there ever can for either of us," he answered, and having said this he rose wearily, and would have passed out through the door but that Dolly stopped him.

"Do not go away without eating something," she said. "We have not much to offer, but still—"

"I cannot eat salt with a woman who feels herself unable to forgive me," he interrupted. "Good-bye, Mrs. Mortomley. I need not tell you to love my wife all the same, for I know she has been staunch to you through every reverse."

And he was gone. Down the walk Dolly watched his retreating figure; along the dusty high-road she watched the man who was ruined pass slowly away, and then she relented. It seemed to come to her in a moment that, in this as in other things, she was but the steward of the man she had married so long as he was unable to see to his affairs for himself, and she knew he would in an instant have held out the right hand of fellowship to Mr. Werner.

I remember once being much impressed by this expression used concerning a girl recently married.

"She is exactly suited to him; but many

men would not care to give their honour into her keeping."

Now this remark had no reference to any divorce scandal possible with the woman. So far as such matters are concerned, any one who had ever known her, might safely have made affidavit she was and would be as utterly without reproach as without fear; but there is another, and if one may say so, without fear of censure, higher sense in which a woman holds her husband's honour in her hand, and that was the sense in which the remark was made.

Just and courteous towards her tradespeople, a gentlewoman in her dealings with servants, not keen and sharp with porters and cab-drivers, considerate to the governess, a stranger within her gates—beyond all things fair in her dealings with her husband's friends—all these points ought not, I think, to be forgotten when one speaks of a man's honour held by a woman.

For truly, she can fail in no single incident I have mentioned without casting a shadow on the judgment of the man who chose her, and it is more than probable Dolly thought this too, for ere Mr. Werner had got a hundred yards from the gate she had sped down the walk, and was flying along the road after him.

" Mr. Werner ! " she cried panting.

And then he stopped and retraced his steps towards her.

" I cannot bear it," she said.

And he noticed she had to sit down on the bank by the wayside to recover her breath.

" I cannot endure, when you are so unhappy, to be hard, as you call it. I know Archie would be vexed if he knew I refused to be friends with you. So please, Mr. Werner, do come back and have some fruit and milk—and I do forgive you from my heart."

" There is something else, Dolly," he observed.

Sooner or later it came natural to all men and all women when nature asserted itself, to call Mortomley's poor Dolly by her Christian name.

"What else?" she asked. "Oh! I re-member, and I am afraid that is a great deal easier. I do hope God will forgive you too, and us all, and I pray he will make you and my dear Lenny very happy in the future."

He stood, with her hand clasped in his, looking at her intently.

"You will not be sorry for this hereafter," he said at last. "When the evil day comes to you which must come to all, you may be glad to remember the words you have spoken this minute. Thank you very, very much. No," he added, in answer to a request that he would return to Wood Cottage; "I have had pleasant tidings spoken to me, and I will leave with their sound in my ears. Good-bye. When you say your prayers to-night do not forget to remember me."

CHAPTER IX.

THE NEW YELLOW.

ALL that night, after saying her prayers—in which she remembered Mr. Werner and his wife, and all other people who were in sore distress—Mrs. Mortomley lay awake, a strange sense of trouble oppressing her.

It was like the old bad times come back again; it was a return of the later evil days at Homewood, to lie in the semi-darkness of the summer night and think of Mr. Werner ruined, Mr. Werner beggared.

How would his wife bear it? Dolly knew her friend pretty well, yet she could not answer this question to her own satisfaction. Mrs. Werner was a noble, generous-hearted,

unselfish woman, and yet Dolly comprehended
in some vague, instinctive sort of way that
wealth and position and social consideration
were very dear to this fresh bankrupt's wife.

There are some people who do not much
care whether they walk or drive through the
world's thoroughfares; indeed, there are those
who, given the choice, would prefer to walk.
Now Mrs. Werner's mind was not so ill-regu-
lated an one as all this comes to. Most emphatically she liked her carriages and horses
and servants, and all the luxuries money can
purchase. She had married for these things,
as Mrs. Mortomley understood perfectly, and
Dolly did not think—no, she did not, that
Leonora would be satisfied to relinquish them.

Further, Mr. Werner had always set himself up as such a model of business capacity
and business prudence, that he really had no
right to fall into difficulties; certainly not to
continue to flounder through difficulties as,
according to his own confession, had been the
case for years.

He had been living a lie, just one of the

things Dolly knew his wife would find it most
difficult to forgive. Had he told her duty
demanded the sacrifice, she might—Mrs. Mortomley understood—have agreed to live in a
house at twenty pounds a year, and wear print
dresses, and be extremely strict about the tea
and sugar, but she could not have done this
with a good grace.

Nevertheless, Dolly believed she could have
borne that better than the consciousness that
the rich raiment she purchased, the luxurious
dinner she provided, the rare wines they drank,
had been paid for by a man all the time virtually bankrupt—a man keeping up an appearance so as to obtain fresh credit, and defer the
striking of that hour of reckoning which could
now be deferred no longer.

Mrs. Mortomley loved Mrs. Werner, and
she did not love Mr. Werner, yet certainly
her sympathies were that night with the man
rather than with the woman.

One's affections are not perhaps strong for
the naughty boy who is always persecuting
one's cat, and stoning one's dog, and slaying

one's chickens, or stealing one's fruit, and yet, when the wicked little wretch comes to grief and goes home with a battered face and cut shins, one's heart is more one with him than with the strong-minded mother, a strict disciplinarian, who we know will lecture or beat him for his sins, as the case may be.

I do not say it is right, for I cannot think it is, that our sympathies should generally be with the evil-doer, but it is very difficult not to feel sorry for the man who, being down, is struck his bitterest blow by those of his own household; and Dolly—well, Dolly did not think if she were in Mr. Werner's shoes she would like to tell the unvarnished truth to Leonora.

Upon the whole Dolly decided he was wise to go abroad, instead of remaining to face the domestic difficulty. "He will write to her," she thought, "tell her all, and she will be very indignant, and think about honour and honesty, and all the rest of it; but she will not, if he is wise, know where to address a letter to him at present. Then she will grow

anxious, both about him and the future of the
children, and at the end of six months I give
her this parcel, when the whole affair is
settled and she need feel no scruples about
taking the money, and then she will feel
touched to remember he thought of her, and
then she will relent and we will find out
where he is; perhaps he may write now and
then to me, and she will go to him, or he will
come back to her, my poor dear Lenny!"

Having completed which pleasing programme of the Werners' future, Mrs. Mortomley ought to have gone to sleep, but she could
not do so, and towards four o'clock she became
so intolerant of her own wakefulness that she
rose and, stealing into the room where Lenore
lay fast asleep, dressed herself noiselessly and
went downstairs, and, letting herself out,
walked across the road and along a footpath
leading to the Lea, which crossed the field in
which stood the shed where she had established her factory.

Not a likely-looking building, and yet it is
in the least pretentious factories that fortunes

are made,—successes won ; and Mrs. Mortomley thanked God every time she looked across
the meadow and beheld the red-tiled roof
which covered the " Hertfordshire Colour
Works" that Lang had so strenuously and—
as it turned out—so wisely advised her to
establish.

The name of Mortomley had a certain power
still, and, though the business letters were
signed in Dolly's scrawl, "D. Mortomley,"
people did not stop to inquire whether it was
an A or a D who was able to supply them
with the colours they required.

Neither was the new company worse
thought of because they were able to supply
so very little.   The public, always liable to be
gulled, did not attribute this to any paucity of
means of production, but rather to the extent
of orders received by the " Hertfordshire
Colour Company."   Acting under Lang's advice, Dolly had taken the business bull by the
horns, and the moment she had settled upon a
residence, a neat circular informed all the
customers whose names Lang could recollect,

or Dolly wring at intervals out of her husband's intermittent memory, that future orders intended for Mortomley and Co. should be addressed to Newham, Herts. Further, she amazed Mr. Swanland by giving directions at the post-office that all letters intended for her husband should be forwarded to that address; and as no fewer than three other persons had applied for the letters, each claiming a right in them, the post-office was somewhat perplexed. First, Mr. Swanland, who, after Dolly had proved to him by chapter and verse that he could claim no letters after the expiration of three months from the meeting of creditors, was forced to strike his flag; secondly, the Thames Street clerk, who had—being trusted by Mr. Swanland—been opening the town letters and suppressing them during the time when the accountant had a right to their possession, and who, so far as I know, is opening and suppressing them to this day; and, third, Hankins, who, being a modified sort of blackguard, made all right with the postmen who delivered at Homewood by representing himself as Mr. Mortomley's chief in absence, and forwarded some letters and retained others.

Dolly never got a tithe of the letters; the battle was one beyond her strength to fight, but it was a battle any accountant worth his salt would have prevented ever being necessary.

Still, in spite of all, the Mortomleys were prospering. The business was a very poor and a very small affair, but, after paying Lang, who was not a cheap coadjutor, and deducting all expenses, Dolly, even in those early days, felt she could safely take a pound a week out of the returns; and, my dear readers, I can assure you that if you have ever known what it is to look nothing a year in the face, you would be very thankful indeed to be able to reckon upon fifty-two pounds as a certainty.

And so Dolly regarded the red-tiled shed gratefully, and did her work in it carefully, for still, as her husband's substitute, she had her work to do. The special amount of water required, the final grains of the special ingredient that shed a lustre over the Mortomley

colours! hers it was to add those trifles which
ensured success. Had the manipulation been
confided to any other, the secret must have
passed out of Mortomley's keeping.

Was not she faithful to her trust! Lang
himself never could tell when the magic touch
was given which illumined the colours they
sent to market. Sometimes in the twilight,
sometimes when the moonbeams streamed
through the skylights, sometimes in the early,
early morning, but always in due and proper
time, Dolly took her slight but all-important
share of the labour, and she did so on the
morning after her interview with Mr. Werner.

As she did so some faint idea that perhaps
he might be able hereafter to help her husband, and her husband help him, crossed her
mind. She did not like Mr. Werner, but she
had a vague comprehension that he was gifted
with some business quality Mortomley lacked,
while Mortomley had capabilities a man such
as Henry Werner might materially assist to
develope.

Already Dolly was beginning to experience that difficulty which always arises when labour goes into partnership with capital. Very faithfully she believed Lang was dealing with her, but he never seemed contented. He never lost an opportunity of letting her know he considered if she would only put full faith in him, the business might be quadrupled.

Jealousy, which is at the root of all strikes, had taken up its abode in Mr. Lang's bosom, and though he tried to avoid giving expression to it, still Mrs. Mortomley knew the fire was there and smouldering.

Like a bad general she kept conceding point after point to keep him in a good humour, and the result was greater dissatisfaction, and less confidence in her fairness of dealing, as week after week rolled by.

She raised his wages, for he had settled wages as a matter of course. She gave him a larger share of the profits; she allowed him unlimited control over the buying and selling; and still Mr. Lang thought himself hardly done by.

He could not say openly he wanted Mrs. Mortomley to place the whole of her husband's formulæ at his discretion, but that was what he really did want; and if he had dared to make the observation, he would have remarked that no woman ought to know so much as Mrs. Mortomley had managed to learn about the process of manufacturing colours.

It was impossible for Dolly not to feel anxious about that future time, when her husband and Lang must come into collision, for she knew perfectly well he ought to have some one on whom he could depend to share the burden with him, and she did not for an instant believe he and her present factotum would be able to stable their horses together, even for a couple of months.

Therefore she could not help considering, that if, when the first trouble and worry were over, Mr. Werner and her husband liked to try to push their fortunes together, she should not feel at all sorry. Lang might have a present of a few recipes, and go away to make a fortune of his own, or he might remain and, under Mr. Werner's stricter discipline, prove more content.

Thinking in a vague rambling sort of way of all these things, Dolly walked slowly along the field-path, a little to the left of which stood the shed, which seemed in her eyes fair as any palace. There was peace in all directions. The fields whence the hay had been carried were glittering with dew, and the cows were lying with the early sun shining upon them, chewing the cud industriously.

At the end of the field flowed the Lea, and a boat was moored to the bank, indicating, as Dolly imagined, the presence of some ardent angler, though she could not discern his whereabouts.

Everything was quiet—so quiet that the stillness of the hour and the scene seemed to lay a quieting hand on Dolly's heart, which was wont sometimes to beat too rapidly and unevenly.

It seemed as if the world and its cares could not come to such a place,—as if there were some virtue of repose in that country

Eden into which the serpent of strife and trouble could not enter.

And so with a light buoyant step Dolly left the main path and tripped along that leading to the shed, styled in pretentious circulars, The Hertfordshire Colour Works.

All at once she stood still, staring like one who did not believe the evidence of her senses, for as she neared the door of the works it was opened cautiously, and a man's face looked out as if reconnoitring.

At sight of Mrs. Mortomley the face was withdrawn, and the door closed with a bang.

For a second Dolly hesitated, and something as like physical fear as she had ever experienced seemed to hold her back. Though within sight of her house, she was utterly unprotected.

There was not a creature within call. There was a man, who certainly had no right on the premises, within the works, and Lang was not likely to appear for another half-hour at any rate.

Nevertheless, after that second's pause

Dolly went on. She pulled out her key and put it in the lock, and found the key would not turn because the lock had been set on the inside. "Open the door whoever you may be," she cried, but there came no answer, only a sound as of some moving about, to which there succeeded a sudden stillness, then a smash of glass, then a rattle of loosened tiles, and finally a man running off as fast as his legs would take him in the direction of the Lea. He jumped into the boat she had seen moored, unloosed his rope, and seizing his oars was fifty yards distant before Mrs. Mortomley could reach the bank of the river.

She retraced her steps to the shed, and sat down beside the door until Lang should arrive.

When he did, his first comment on the affair was—

"You'll get yourself murdered one of these nights or mornings, ma'am, coming out all alone with no soul to help you if any one had a mind to do you harm."

"I shall have protection with me for the

future," she said calmly. "Now, what do you suppose that man was doing here?"

"He was after the Yellow," pronounced Mr. Lang solemnly. "There'll be many a one after that now it has gone to market. There'll be people, I know, who wouldn't mind standing five hundred pounds if they could only buy our process. Like enough that fellow has burst open the drawer and gone away with the receipt."

"I do not think that very likely, as I never leave a paper of any importance in the drawer," Dolly answered.

"Well, if you carry that receipt about with you I should not care, if I was in your place, about coming across these fields alone."

"Don't talk nonsense, Lang," was the reply, "but go and get a ladder and open the door, and let us see what the man has really been doing."

When the door was opened, they found Lang's prophecy fulfilled. The drawer was broken open and all the parcels it contained abstracted.

"I'll be bound the fellow has spoiled all our colours too," remarked Mr. Lang, but in this he chanced to be mistaken. Their colours then in process of making turned out as good as ever.

"I wouldn't for fifty pounds this had happened," remarked Lang.

"Nor I, for five times fifty," Mrs. Mortomley answered; and without uttering another word, she walked slowly and thoughtfully back to Wood Cottage.

CHAPTER X.

A BROKEN REED.

THAT morning's post brought with it a letter from Miss Gerace, which bore on the envelope these words :—

"IMMEDIATE DELIVERY IS REQUESTED."

"What on earth can be the matter with my aunt now?" thought Dolly as she opened it.

Next moment Lenore called out, "Mamma, mamma!" and Esther, happening to be bringing in the kettle at that instant, exclaimed, "Oh! ma'am, what has happened?"

But Dolly put them both aside, and sitting down all of a tremble, spread the letter on the table, for her hands were shaking so she could not hold it steady, and read to herself,

" Dreadful news has reached us to-night ; a telegram to say *Mr. Werner is dead.* Leonora is like one distracted, and poor Mrs. Trebasson completely prostrated. Leonora left by the express, and I write to entreat you to go to her at once. We forgot to ask her Lord Darsham's present address. Get it and tele-graph to him immediately. Mrs. Trebasson wishes me to go to London to see if I can be of any use, so I shall see you soon. Do not lose a moment in going to Leonora.

" Yours,

" A. G."

Dolly rose up like a person who had re-ceived some dreadful blow.

" Fetch me my hat and shawl, Esther," she said. " I must go to London by the next train."

" But you have not had any breakfast ma'am," expostulated the girl.

Mrs. Mortomley made no reply. She only walked through the open door and began pacing up and down the plot of grass.

Lenore ran after her crying, "My dear, dear mamma, what is the matter?" and Esther followed with "Oh! my dear mistress, speak to me."

"Mrs. Werner is in great trouble, and I must go to her. Do not ask me anything more," was the reply, and then Dolly leaned up against a great tree growing in the hedgerow, and shut her eyes, and felt as if the earth were going round and round. She understood, if no one else did,—she comprehended that of his own free will Henry Werner had gone on the longest and darkest journey the human mind can imagine —that his message to his wife would be given from one who sent it, knowing ere eight hours of the six months had elapsed he would have passed into eternity. This was why he had spoken so freely to her, and this was the reason he had extorted her forgiveness, and asked her to remember him in her prayers. Every other consideration in life was for the moment blotted out by the shadow of that man dead—dead by his own act—dead because the trouble was too great to be contended with, because the ruin was too utter to be endured.

Dolly went upstairs. She had paused by the way and swallowed some wine and water, to enable her tongue to perform its office.

"Archie," she said, as she nervously smoothed her husband's pillows, "I must go to London, and I want you to be quiet and satisfied while I am away. Leonora is in dreadful distress, and wants me. Mr. Werner is dangerously ill, not expected to recover, and she has great need of me. I do not like leaving you, dear, but—"

"Go at once," he interrupted. "Kiss me and go, dear. I shall do very well indeed. Poor Werner! It is a curious thing I was dreaming about him yesterday. I dreamt he was here, and—"

"I must go, love," she said, unable to bear the interview longer. "Good-bye."

And she was gone.

Now it so happened that Mrs. Mortomley chanced, without any reference to Mrs. Werner, to know Lord Darsham's then address, and consequently the moment she got into town she telegraphed this message to him.

" Leonora's husband has committed suicide. Pray come to her at once."

Mrs. Mortomley only sent this message because she considered that, by stating what she believed to be the literal truth, she would bring Leonora's cousin more rapidly to her assistance. In the then state of her nerves, sudden death by the Visitation of God seemed to her so slight a misfortune that she fancied pure death would appear a trifle to Lord Darsham.

That any one could ever really have supposed Mr. Werner died through illness or misadventure, never occurred to Dolly, who felt quite positive he had fully made up his mind to destroy himself when with her on the preceding day, and it was therefore with a frightful shock she learned upon arriving at her friend's house that every soul in it believed Mr. Werner, who was suffering from a severe attack of neuralgia, had died accidentally while inhaling chloroform to lull the pain.

" What a dreadful thing I have done!" she thought. " How shall I ever be able to make it right with Lord Darsham ? "

And then Dolly went upstairs into that very room where Mr. and Mrs. Werner had held their colloquy about the Mortomleys, and found Mrs. Werner as nearly insane as a rational woman can ever be.

She was full of self-reproach, and Dolly thanked God for it. Knowing what she knew of the man's misery, it would have tried her almost beyond endurance to have listened to the faintest whisper of self-pity, but there was none.

Nothing save sorrow for the husband, taken so suddenly, for his children left orphaned, for the years during which she might have made him happier.

"I thought myself a good wife," she moaned, "but I was not a good wife. I helped him as I imagined, but, Dolly dear, an ounce of love is worth a pound of pride any day. He wanted, he must have wanted, something more when he returned to this great cold, handsome house than a woman to sit at the head of his dinner table. I have thought about it all at Dassell, Dolly darling. I made up my mind, God helping me, to be more a wife to him

than I had ever been, and it is all too late—
too late—too late."

" I am afraid he had a great deal on his
mind," Dolly ventured.

"Yes, there can be no doubt about that.
He was so fond of business, and thought so
much of money, and—"

" We won't talk about it, dear, now," Mrs.
Mortomley said softly.

" Have you—seen him?" Mrs. Werner
asked, after a pause.

"No," Dolly answered. " I should like to
do so, though, if I may."

" You have quite forgiven him?"

" I had done that, Lenny, thank God, before
this."

Just a faint pressure of the trembling fingers, and Dolly rose to go downstairs.

"Williams, I want to see your master," she
said, and Williams forthwith conducted her
into the same room where Messrs. Forde and
Kleinwort had sat on that night when they
came to Mr. Werner's house in quest of Mortomley.

There in the same dress he wore when last she saw him alive, he lay stiff and dead.

"Why has not something been done with him?" Dolly asked shuddering. "Why do you let him lie there like that?"

"We must not move him until after the inquest," said the man.

Mrs. Mortomley crept upstairs again—in her folly what had she done?

But for her this inquest might have passed over quietly, and a verdict of killed by an accidental dose of chloroform returned.

The hours of that day lengthened themselves into years, and when at last Miss Gerace arrived, she found her niece looking the picture of death itself.

"My dear child, you must go home," she said, gazing in shocked amazement at Dolly's changed face and figure. "All this is too much for you."

But Dolly said, "No; if you love me, aunt, go to Wood Cottage and take care of Archie till I can leave Leonora. I must see the end of it. I will tell you why some day. I cannot leave now."

So Miss Gerace went to Wood Cottage, and wrapping her bonnet in a handkerchief laid it on the drawers in Lenore's room, and so solemnly set up her Lares and Penates in Dolly's house, and she broke the news of Mr. Werner's sudden death wisely and calmly to Mr. Mortomley, who turned his head from the light and lay very still and quiet, thinking mighty solemn thoughts for an hour afterwards.

"I think my poor Dolly ought not to stay there," he said at last. "She has had trouble enough of her own to bear lately."

"And I think your Dolly is at this moment just where God means her to be," answered Miss Gerace, a little gruffly, for she herself was uneasy about her niece's appearance, and in her heart considered Dolly stood in as much need of tender care as Mrs. Werner.

Just about the time when Miss Gerace was leaving, in order to make the to her unaccustomed journey to London, Mr. Forde sat alone in his office waiting impatiently for

the appearance of Werner, or a note from
him.

" You shall hear from me to-morrow before
midday, without fail," Werner had promised
on the previous forenoon, and whatever his
faults he had never failed in a promise of this
nature before.

" Ah ! if that little wretch Kleinwort, who
loved always to be talking evil about Werner,
had only been like him, I need never have
been reduced to the straits in which I find
myself to-day," thought the unfortunate
manager.

" Had any one planted an acre of reeds, Mr.
Forde would have gone on transferring his
simple faith from one to another till the last
one broke." So Henry Werner declared ; and
no person understood so well as he that when
his collapse ensued, the last poor reed on
which the manager leaned would be broken to
pieces.

That very morning when Mr. Forde waited
for his constituents, as for some reason best
known to himself he had latterly began to call

the customers of the General Chemical Company, he had gone through one of those interviews with his directors, which, to quote his own phrase, "made him feel old," and he had pretty good grounds for believing that if Henry Werner, the last big card in his hand, failed to win him a trick he could not stay at St. Vedast Wharf.

In that case all must come out. The shareholders would begin to ask troublesome questions which the directors must answer; and he —well—he, with all his heart and soul wished when he put on his hat over Mortomley's affairs, he had kept it on and left St. Vedast Wharf for ever, shaking the dust off his shoes as he did so.

But now all he had to hope for was that Henry Werner would obey his commands, issued in no doubtful terms, and bring that which might satisfy his, Mr. Forde's, directors.

Werner had ordered him out of his office, indeed, words grew so high between them; but he had still said he should be heard of by midday, and now it was one o'clock and neither he nor any tidings had come.

Mr. Forde felt he could not endure being treated in this way any longer, so he walked across to Mr. Werner's office, where he asked young Carless, once in Mortomley's Thames Street Warehouse, if his master was in.

"He has not come yet," was the answer; and had Mr. Forde been looking at the clerks' faces instead of thinking of Mr. Werner's shortcomings, he would have noticed an expression on them which might well have puzzled his comprehension.

"I will wait for him," and Mr. Forde made a step towards the inner office as if intending to take up a position there.

"Better sit down here," said one of the senior clerks, offering him a chair; "the inner office is locked."

"Locked! who locked it?" asked Mr. Forde angrily.

"Mr. Werner, when he left yesterday," was the reply.

Ten minutes passed, quarter of an hour struck, then the manager said,

"It does not seem of much use my waiting

here. Tell Mr. Werner to come round to me the instant he arrives—the instant, remember. What are you looking at each other for in that manner ? " he continued, shouting at them passionately. " Do you mean to do what I tell you or not ? "

All the clerks but one drew back a little abashed ; they had silently countenanced the perpetration of a grim practical joke, which, while the clock went on ticking, seemed to grow flat and stale and unprofitable to each of them save Carless.

He it was who now answered.

" Perhaps you are not aware that our governor is dead."

" You had better take care, sir," said Mr. Forde. " I do not know whether Mr. Werner has granted you a licence for impertinence, but if he has—by — he shall rue it and you too."

" It is true though," interposed a man sitting in a dark part of the office, who had not hitherto spoken, but remained, his head supported by his hands, reading ' The Times.'

" What is true," demanded the manager.

"That Mr. Werner is dead. I had occasion to go to his house this morning and found that he died last night."

"It is a lie; it is a —— put off. He is gone like that villain Kleinwort; but he need not think to escape me. I will find him if he is above ground?"

"You won't have far to go then," was the reply. "He is lying stiff and safe enough in his own study."

"And he is gone to a land with which we have no extradition treaty," observed Carless, as Mr. Forde banged the door behind him.

"Hold your tongue, do," entreated the 'Times'' student, who, having been in a fashion confidential clerk to Mr. Werner, had some comprehension how the matter stood. "Our governor has been badgered into his grave, and I only hope they will call me on the inquest that I may be able to state my belief."

"And he was not half a bad sort, the governor," said Carless, shutting up the day-book.

"I say let's all go to the funeral," suggested a third; and so these young men wrote their employer's epitaph.

Meantime Mr. Forde was proceeding westward as fast as the legs of a swift horse could take him. To describe what he felt would be as impossible as to detail the contents and occupants of each vehicle the hansom passed— the hopes and fears — the miseries and joys hidden behind the walls of the countless houses, which lay to left and right of his route.

He believed; he did not believe. He dreaded; no it was all a sham. Now in imagination he started himself with the detectives in pursuit, again with dry parched lips he was answering the questions of his directors.

If he had realized the fact, he suffered in the course of that rapid drive enough misery to have driven many a man insane. Misery of his own causing if you will, but misery all the harder to endure on that account.

Happily for himself, however, Mr. Forde was a person who did not realize. He was a man who before he had grasped the worst decided there must be some means of escape from it, and accordingly, the first words he uttered to Williams were—

"Now, then, what's all this?"

"Have not you heard, sir," answered that well-trained functionary, startled for once out of his propriety of demeanour by Mr. Forde's tremendous knock, by Mr. Forde's loud utterance, "my master died last night!"

"Died! Nonsense; went away you mean."

"Passed away, sir, if you prefer that expression," acquiesced the man. "He had been out all day, and when he returned in the evening he said it was of no use serving dinner, for he was suffering such agonies from neuralgia that he could not eat anything. He had called at the doctor's on his way, but he was not at home.

"He asked me to bring him a cup of strong coffee, which I did.

"About eight o'clock I went in to the study to light the gas, and when I opened the door there was a strong smell of some apothecary's stuff," (here the man became visibly affected), "and something in that and the way my master was lying on the sofa attracted my attention. I spoke to him, but he did not answer me. I lifted his arm which was hanging over on the carpet, but it fell again when I let it go.

"Then I ran out of the house for a doctor. I had seen a doctor's carriage standing at the next door. He came in and looked at him. I asked what could be done, and he said 'Nothing, the poor gentleman is dead.'"

"Where is he?" asked Mr. Forde, who had listened impatiently to this statement.

"In the study, sir."

Mr. Forde crossed the hall and turned the handle of the door, but the door was locked.

"Have you the key?" he asked. "Yes, sir," answered Williams, fumbling in his pocket nervously—the fact being that, notwithstanding his large experience of the world and knowledge of society, he had never before come in contact with any one who did not consider it necessary at all events, to assume a certain sympathy with misfortune, and it is no exaggeration to say Mr. Forde's utter callousness frightened the man.

He had never previously seen a human being whose intense thought for self swallowed up every thought for other people; to whom the death or ruin of any number of his fellow-creatures was simply a bagatelle when compared with any misfortune which could touch himself.

"If you cannot unlock the door, let me do it," remarked Mr. Forde, taking the key out of Williams' fingers, and shooting back the bolt with a quick sharp click; with a steady determined step he crossed the room.

"Raise that blind," he said.

Williams hesitated, but then obeyed, and at the same moment Mr. Forde drew aside, with no faltering or gentle touch, the handker-chief which covered the dead man's face.

There he lay, as he had died. There was no sneer curling the lip now, no scowl disfiguring the forehead. There was no expression of despair, no look of anguish. Death was fast smoothing the hard lines out of that dark face;

and as Mr. Forde realized all this—realized there was no deception about the matter—that no insult could reach his sense, no dread affect him more, he could have cursed the man who long and long before had told him if ever misfortune came upon him he should know how to meet it. This was how he had met it; this was what he had in his mind then. Mr. Forde understood perfectly that when once he found the battle going against him, when once he found the tide setting too strongly for him to resist its flow, he had always meant to end the difficulty thus.

" Yes, he is dead sure enough," commented Mr. Forde at length. " He has taken precious good care to leave other people in the lurch as any one who ever knew Henry Werner might safely have sworn he would do."

" I do not quite understand, sir," said the butler deprecatingly.

" Oh ! you don't, my friend. Well, perhaps not ; perhaps you think your master really had neuralgia, and really took that stuff to cure it."

" Certainly, sir."

" Oh ! you do, do you ?   Well, then, I can
tell you, the coward took it because he was afraid
to meet his creditors, because he was afraid to
meet ME, because he knew he was a beggar,
and that if he did not do something of this
sort, his fine feathers would be stripped off,
and he and his turned out into the world
without a shilling, as better people have been
before now.

" I must see his wife before I leave," he
added abruptly.

" See Mrs. Werner, sir ?   Impossible."

" Impossible ! Why is it impossible ? Who
is she that she should not be seen ; who is she
that she should not hear what I have to say ?
She has had all the smooth, she must now take
her share of the rough."

" My mistress, sir, is very ill," remarked
Williams, who really was in a state of mind
baffling description.

He believed Mr. Forde was mad, but he
could not determine how to get him out of the
house.

"Ill," repeated Mr. Forde; "and so am I very ill, yet I have to be about. I shall have to face my directors to-morrow over that villain's affairs. Sick or well I shall have to be in the City. Don't talk to me about illness. I must and I will see Mrs. Werner, and you may go and tell her so."

"If you will please to walk into the dining-room, sir, I will deliver your message," said the butler. He really was afraid of leaving Mr. Forde alone with the corpse, uncertain whether, in default of the living man, he might not wreak his vengeance on the dead, and it was with a gasp of relief he saw Mr. Forde out of the study, and locked the door behind him.

"Ask Mrs. Mortomley to speak to me for a minute," he whispered to Mrs. Werner's maid, and when Dolly came to him on the landing, he told her all Mr. Forde had said.

Dolly listened to the end, then she answered,

"Tell Mr. Forde from me, that if he waits in this house for ever, he shall never speak to Mrs. Werner, but that if he has any communication to make, Lord Darsham will see him this evening at eight o'clock."

Downstairs went Williams with this message, which Dolly, leaning over the banisters, heard him deliver in less curt language.

"I know nothing of Lord Darsham," answered Mr. Forde, walking up and down the hall. "I have had no transactions with him, but I have with that fellow," an intimation indicating Werner lying dead in the study. "He has robbed us, and ruined me, and by — I will see his wife."

"Williams," rang out Dolly's voice at this juncture, clear and shrill, and yet with an undertone of intensified passion in it, "if that person insists on remaining in a house where there is so much misery, send for a policeman. I will take the responsibility."

And forthwith Dolly retreated to Mrs. Werner's dressing-room, and bolted the doors of that and her friend's apartment.

She had once been brave, but the days and the weeks and the months had been draining her courage. Physically, she felt she was not strong enough to encounter one of the people who had compassed her husband's ruin; and though she would have fought for Leonora till she died, still her woman's nature warned her to shun a fight if possible.

"You will go now please, sir," urged poor Williams, "and come back and see his lordship to-night."

Whereupon Mr. Forde anathematized his lordship, and asked,

"How does that woman, that wife of Mortomley's, come here?"

"She was sent for, sir; my mistress has been quieter since her arrival. They are old friends."

"Humph," ejaculated Mr. Forde; "then any fool can tell where Henry Werner's money went." And he permitted himself to be edged out to the door-step by Williams, who took an early opportunity of saying he was wanted and of shutting the door hastily on that unwelcome visitor.

All that afternoon Williams surveyed callers doubtfully from a side window before opening the door. Had Mr. Forde again appeared, he would have put up the chain, and parleyed with him like a beleagured city to the opposing force.

About six o'clock Lord Darsham came rattling up in a hansom. He had telegraphed back a reply to Dolly, and followed that reply as fast as an express train could bring him.

She ran downstairs, thankful for his arrival, and after years, long, long years, the Vicar of Dassell's little girl and Charley Trebasson, Leonora's first lover, met again.

"I should have known you anywhere," he said, after the first words of greeting and exclamations of pity and horror were uttered.

"Am I so little changed?" she asked, with a forced smile.

"Ah! you are so much changed," he answered; "you look so many years too old, you look so much too thin. What is the matter with you Mrs. Mortomley? I cannot bear to —"

"Never mind me," she said almost brusquely; "Your business now is with Leonora; I ought not to have sent you that telegram, you must forget it."

"Is Mr. Werner not dead then?" he asked.

"Dead! yes, indeed he is poor fellow!" she answered; "but I acted on a fancy when I telegraphed that he committed suicide. He took chloroform to relieve the pain of neuralgia, and the chloroform killed him."

Mrs. Werner's cousin looked Mrs. Mortomley steadily in the face while she uttered this sentence, then, when she paused and hesitated, he said,

"You had better be perfectly frank with me. I remember, if you do not, how when you were a child, it was of no use your trying to tell a fib because your eyes betrayed you, and I must say to you now, as I often said to you then, speak the truth, for with that tell-tale face no one will believe you when you try to invent a likely falsehood."

"To be perfectly straightforward then," answered Dolly; "when I sent that telegram to you I believed Mr. Werner had destroyed himself; when I arrived here, I found every one believed his death was due entirely to accident."

"And may I inquire why you believed he had committed suicide ? "

"No," she replied; " that is my secret, and for very special reasons I want to have nothing to do with the matter—special reasons, " she repeated; " not selfish, pray understand. I did not think of the inquest; I did not think of anything except that, on Leonora's account, you ought to be here, when I wrote that telegram, and — "

" I know what you mean," he interrupted; seeing the subject affected her deeply, and he took a turn up and down the room before he spoke again.

" What could have induced him to kill himself?" he said, at length stopping abruptly in his walk.

"A Mr. Forde, who has been here to-day, demanding to see Leonora, and who is coming this evening to see you, told Williams he was afraid to meet his creditors. Williams, who has never seen the slightest evidence of shortness of money about this house, inclines to the opinion that Mr. Forde is mad, and I have done my best to confirm that opinion, but Mr. Forde I believe to be right; I am afraid you will find he destroyed himself, because he was a ruined man."

There was silence for a minute, broken only by the sound of Dolly's suppressed sobs.

"Poor fellow," said Lord Darsham; he must have suffered horribly before it came to this."

"Only those who have gone through such an ordeal can imagine what he must have endured," she answered simply; "depend upon it his heart was broken days before he died."

"I never liked Werner," commented her auditor. "I always thought him a self-contained money-worshiping snob, and I never believed, spite of the purple and fine linen, that Leonora was happy in her marriage, but I am sorry for him now. A man who commits suicide must have an enormous capacity for misery, and a man who has an enormous capacity for misery must have had an enormous capacity for something better, had any opportunity for developing it occurred."

"You will forget my telegram," she entreated.

"I shall say nothing about it, which will amount to much the same thing," he answered.

CHAPTER XI.

TWO UNWELCOME VISITORS.

THE business of living goes on all the same let who will retire from active participation in it, and, accordingly, Mrs. Mortomley and Lord Darsham sat down to dinner, although the whilom master of the house lay dead in that small room on the other side the hall, where he had made his exit from this world. But, in truth, that dinner was a very funereal affair. There was a something ghastly in eating of the ruined man's substance; in drinking of the wines he had selected; in occupying the apartment where he must often have sat at table with a guest no one else could see facing him; and the conversation in Williams's pre-

sence, compulsorily of no private nature,
flagged as conversation did not often flag
when Dolly held one of the battledores.

With great persuasion Mrs. Werner had
been induced to swallow a draught ordered
for her by the family physician, and she lay
in a sleep as sound and almost as dreamless as
that which enfolded the silent figure lying all
alone in the twilight of the summer's evening.

Thirty hours before, he was alive ; and now,
his spirit had started on the long, lonesome
journey ; and through the gloom of the Valley
of the Shadow no human eye could follow
him.

Dolly could not get over the horror of it
all ; and when Mr. Forde's knock woke the
echoes of the house, she started from her seat
in an access of terror, and exclaiming,

"Oh! let me get upstairs before he comes
in," left the room, and ran upstairs to Mrs.
Werner's apartment.

Meanwhile, Williams, before answering the
summons, inquired whether his Lordship

would be pleased to see the expected visitor, and if so, where.

"Yes," was the answer; "show him in here."

Mr. Forde entered. He had employed the interval between his two visits in alternating between two opinions. One, that Henry Werner would come to life again; the other, that Lord Darsham would wipe off the deceased's indebtedness to the St. Vedast Wharf Company.

As the last would be by far the most satisfactory result to him, he finally decided that a miracle would not be wrought in Henry Werner's favour, but that Lord Darsham would pay, which Mr. Forde decided would be better than a miracle.

Full of this idea, he entered the room with so subdued an expression, and so deferential a manner, and so sympathising a face, that Lord Darsham, who had heard Williams's account of his demeanour a few hours previously, could scarcely believe the evidence of his eyes.

"Sad affair this, my Lord," remarked Mr. Forde when Williams, having placed a chair for the visitor, had left the room.

"My Lord" agreed that it was a very sad affair.

"Particularly under the circumstances, my Lord," proceeded Mr. Forde.

"My Lord" thought that sudden death under any circumstances must always be regarded as very awful.

"And when a man dies by his own act—" Mr. Forde was commencing, when Lord Darsham stopped him.

"Pardon me for interrupting you," he said, "but will you kindly inform me upon what circumstance you ground your opinion that Mr. Werner did die by his own act?"

"The state of his affairs, my Lord."

"Are his affairs embarrassed?"

"If you are not aware of the fact, my Lord, you are fortunate; for that proves he is not in your Lordship's debt."

"He certainly owes me no money," was the reply. "But all this is not an answer to my question. I entirely fail to see the connection between his death and his debts. Is it a usual thing in the City for a mau to kill himself when he finds he cannot pay his way?"

"Not usual, my Lord; but still, such things are; and when one hears a man in difficulties has taken chloroform for neuralgia, and is found dead in consequence, one draws one's own conclusions."

"Well, I do not know," said the other thoughtfully; "but it seems to me very hard that because a man owes money any one should imagine he has thought it necessary to destroy himself. Mr. Werner, I imagine, was not destitute of friends who would have been willing to assist him; at all events, Mrs. Werner was not. To the utmost of their ability, I think I may say, all her relations would have helped her husband had they been aware of his embarrassments."

"That remark does you honour, my Lord. The sentiment is precisely what I should have expected to hear you utter. In fact, I felt so satisfied you would wish, for Mrs. Werner's sake, to keep this matter quiet, that, at some inconvenience to myself, I ran up this evening to talk the affair over."

"He is coming to some point now; he has, in his eagerness, forgotten to milord me," thought Mrs. Werner's cousin, and he said aloud,

"I am much obliged; it was very kind and thoughtful of you, Mr. Forde."

"Don't mention it, I beg, my Lord," replied that gentleman. "Anything I could do to serve you or Mrs. Werner would give me the greatest pleasure. It is a very sad thing —very sad, indeed; but I think the affair can be kept quiet if I tell my directors you are prepared to meet their claims upon Mr. Werner. I do not wish to be troublesome, but I think if you gave me a scrap of writing to that effect (the merest line would do, just to prove that what I say is all *bonâ fide*), it might make matters easier."

Lord Darsham stared at the speaker in unfeigned amazement.

"I am utterly at a loss to understand your meaning," he said.

"I merely meant that, as it is your Lordship's honourable intention to wipe off Mr.
Werner's liability to our firm, the sooner my
directors are satisfied on that point, the better
it will be for every one concerned."

"I have not the slightest intention of paying any of Mr. Werner's debts," was the
reply. "I cannot imagine what could have
induced you to leap to such a conclusion."

"Your own words, my Lord—your own
words!" retorted Mr. Forde, growing a little
hot. "Your Lordship said distinctly that had
Mrs. Werner's relations, amongst whom of
course I reckon your Lordship, been aware of
Mr. Werner's embarrassments, he would have
received substantial assistance from the
family."

"So he would," agreed Lord Darsham.
"Had assistance been possible, we should have
given it."

"Then it follows as a matter of course, my
Lord, that so far as lies in your Lordship's
power you will like to save his honour by paying his debts."

"Such a deduction follows by no means," said Lord Darsham decidedly. "We should have been very glad for Mrs. Werner's sake to assist her husband; but we cannot assist him now. It is impossible we should have the slightest interest in his creditors, and I can say most emphatically they will never receive one penny from me."

"Do you consider this honourable conduct, my Lord?" asked Mr. Forde.

"Decidedly I do. While Mr. Werner was living we should have been willing to help him, as I have already stated; now he is dead, he is beyond the possibility of help."

"Now he is dead, it is a very easy thing for your Lordship to say you would have helped him had he been living," observed Mr. Forde tauntingly, with the nearest approach to a sneer of which his features were capable.

Lord Darsham made no reply. He only smiled, and taking a fern from the basket nearest to where he sat, laid it on the cloth and contemplated its tracery.

"Am I to understand that it is your Lord-

ship's deliberate determination to do nothing?"
asked Mr. Forde after a, to him, heart-breaking
pause.

"I shall certainly not pay his debts, if that
is what you mean," was the reply.

Mr. Forde sat silent for a moment. He
could scarcely believe in such depravity. He
had thought some degree of right and proper
feeling prevailed amongst the aristocracy, and
now here was a lord, a creature who happened
to be a lord, who deliberately said he would
not pay Henry Werner's liabilities to the
General Chemical Company, Limited!

At length he said,

"Perhaps your Lordship is not aware that
this is a very serious matter to me?"

"I am very sorry to hear it," was the reply,
but Lord Darsham did not look in the least
sorry.

"If your Lordship will do nothing to enable
me to tide over the anger of my directors, I
shall have to leave, and what will become of
my wife and children I cannot imagine. Your
Lordship ought to consider them and me;

brought to beggary through the misconduct and cowardice of your relative. Your Lordship will see me safe through this matter?" he finished entreatingly.

"Mr. Forde," said his Lordship very gravely and very decidedly, "I wish you would take my 'no' as final. In the first place, Mr. Werner was not my relative; in the second, he is dead; in the third, if his affairs should prove to be in the hopeless state you indicate, I shall have to maintain his wife and family; and in the fourth, a man who violates decency towards the dead and respect towards the living by using such language as you thought fit to employ when speaking to-day to a servant, must be held to have forfeited all claim to pity and consideration if he ever possessed any."

"Why, what did I say?" inquired Mr. Forde.

Incredible as it may seem, he retained no recollection of having used any phrase capable of giving the slightest offence. He had but one idea—money—and of how he expressed

himself when trying to get it or when he
found he had lost it, he had no more remem-
brance than a man of his utterances in de-
lirium.

"If your memory is so bad you must not
come to me to refresh it," answered Lord
Darsham. "I will only say that the next
time you wish to propitiate a man's friends, it
may be more prudent for you not to open proceedings by telling his servants he is a coward,
who has committed suicide because he feared
to meet his creditors."

"That was true though," explained Mr.
Forde.

"You are not in a position to know whether
it is true or false," was the reply; "but whether
true or false, it was a most unseemly observation."

"I am the best judge of that, sir!" retorted Mr. Forde, rising as Lord Darsham rose,
and buttoning his coat up. "And when all
comes out about Henry Werner which must
come out, you will be sorry you did not try to
come to some sort of a settlement with me. I

hold his forged acceptances for thousands, sir— thousands ! I held him in the hollow of my hand. I could have transported him any hour, but I refrained, and this is all I get for my forbearance. I will make your ears tingle yet, my Lord Darsham."

Without answering a word, Lord Darsham walked to the fireplace and rang the bell, which Williams answered with unwonted celerity.

" Show Mr. Forde out," said Mrs. Werner's cousin, " and never let him enter the house again."

" You do not mean it, my Lord ; you cannot," urged the unfortunate believer in human reeds, with a desperation which was almost pathetic. " You will do something in the matter ; you will think over it. Consider my wife and children."

" Mr. Forde, I have nothing to do, and I will have nothing to do, with you or your wife or your children."

Lord Darsham's tone was as conclusive as his words. Nevertheless, Mr. Forde would have clung to this last straw, and shown him still more reasons why he should make all right with his directors, had not Williams taken him by the arm and half pushed, half dragged him to the front door, and thrust him without ceremony out into the night.

"I really think the best thing I could do would be to go and drown myself," he thought, as he looked up at the window of the room where Henry Werner lay dead; but he was not of the stuff suicides are made of.

He neither drowned nor hanged himself, swallowed poison nor cut his throat. He went home and slept upon his trouble instead.

To Mrs. Mortomley's relief, the coroner's inquest, held to find out the why and wherefore attending Mr. Werner's decease, resulted in a verdict of "Accidental Death." The jury, it is perhaps unnecessary to state, added a recommendation that chloroform should never be inhaled save under the advice and in the presence of a medical man.

What good purpose they proposed to effect by this advice was known only to themselves, but the next day it appeared in all the dignity of print in the daily papers, and was in due time copied from them into the country papers, and so read in London and throughout the provinces by all whom it might or might not concern.

Whatever Williams' opinion of Mr. Forde's utterances might be, after a night's reflection he was too discreet a servant to give utterance to it, and consequently his statements were perfectly satisfactory to jurymen and coroner alike. The City and the West End were so far apart that not a whisper of embarrassment had reached the ears of the two doctors who gave evidence in the case. The dead man had been far too astute to leave even a scrap of writing indicating his design, and it was with a feeling of no common satisfaction that Lord Darsham, after that anxious hour was over, gave an attendant undertaker audience, and instructed him to provide a strictly private funeral for the morning next but one following.

Having done this, he walked with a lighter heart to his hotel, having told Mrs. Mortom-

ley he would see her again the following day,
but he had not left the house ten minutes before a man sprucely dressed, jaunty in manner,
fluent of speech, assured as to demeanour, rang
at the visitors' bell and asked to see Mr.
Werner.

"Mr. Werner is dead," answered Williams,
looking doubtfully at the new-comer, who wore
a geranium in his coat, and used a toothpick
freely during the interview.

"I heard something about that. Awkward,
ain't it?" remarked the free-and-easy individual. "I'll have to see Mrs. Werner, that
is all," he added, after a moment's pause.

"My mistress cannot see any one," Williams
replied, closing the door about an inch, as he
saw an intention on the stranger's part of entering uninvited.

The other laughed, and put his foot on the
threshold.

"Not so fast, my friend," he said. "I have
come concerning a little matter which must be
attended to immediately. We can talk about
it more at our ease inside," and with a quick

and unexpected movement he put Williams on one side and stood within the hall. "That is all right," he said, drawing his breath with a sigh of relief. "Now I want half a year's rent, that is my business."

"There is no one here who can attend to any business at present," replied Williams. "My master is lying dead in the house. The funeral is to be the day after to-morrow. My mistress has not left her room since yesterday morning, and Lord Darsham has just gone to his hotel."

"Then you had better send to his hotel after him," answered the visitor, sitting down on one of the hall chairs and commencing music-hall reminiscences by softly whistling a negro melody through his teeth.

Now, it is a fact, Williams had not the faintest idea who or what this man really was. He had lived all his life, if not in the best families, at least in families that paid their way, and knew nothing of duns or writs, or summonses or sheriff's officers, and he, therefore, stood looking in astonishment, not unmixed with indignation, at the gentleman possessed of musical proclivities till that person, out of patience with his hesitation, exclaimed,

"Now then, stupid, are you going to send for that lord you were speaking of, or are you not? I can't wait here all day while you are making up your small brains into a big parcel. If you don't look sharp I must leave a man in possession, and I don't expect your people would thank you much for that."

"Will you tell me what you mean?" Williams entreated.

First the death, then Mr. Forde, then this —it was too much experience thrust upon him all at once.

"I mean," said the other, speaking very slowly, and looking very intently at Williams from under the brim of his hat, which was tilted well over his eyes, "that I am sent here to get two quarters' rent, and that I must either have it or leave a man in charge of enough to cover the amount. So now you had better see about the getting the money, for I ain't agoing to waste my blessed time here much longer for any man living or dead— Lords or Commons."

And he rose as if to give emphasis to his words, rose and yawned and stretched himself, after which performances he sat down again.

"If you wait for a few minutes I will see what can be done," said Williams, his thoughts turning in this dire extremity to Mrs. Mortomley.

"I'll wait, never fear," answered the other; and he took a newspaper from his pocket and began to read it with a nonchalant manner which fairly appalled the butler.

Dolly was sitting alone in the great drawing-room, that which Mr. Werner had furnished so gorgeously after his own taste—a taste Mrs. Mortomley always considered vile, when Williams came quietly in.

"I beg your pardon, ma'am, but a most unpleasant thing has occurred, and I thought it better to mention it to you. A person is below who says he wants two quarters' rent, and that he must have it."

"I do not know where or from whom he is to get it then," remarked Mrs. Mortomley, lifting her heavy eyes from the book she was reading.

"But—excuse me, ma'am, I hardly like to repeat his words, only I really do not know how to get rid of him. He says he must leave a man in possession if he is not paid immediately."

"If he must we cannot prevent him," Dolly answered. She had gone through it all. She understood this was the beginning of the end for her friend Leonora, and she felt no good could possible accrue from exciting herself about the matter.

Not so Williams; fortunately he attributed Mrs. Mortomley's indifference to non-comprehension, otherwise her *sang froid* would have shocked him beyond measure. Personally he felt he could scarcely outlive the degradation of being in the house with a bailiff. He was willing to make any exertion, to endure any sacrifice, to avert so great a calamity.

"Had not I better go for his Lordship?" he suggested.

"You can if you like," she answered; "but I do not think your doing so can serve any good purpose. In the first place you may not find Lord Darsham at his hotel ; in the second, I do not believe this man would wait till you could return. Then, these people never will take a cheque, and it is long past bank hours, and finally, I very much doubt whether Lord Darsham ought to pay any account until he has seen Mr. Werner's lawyers."

Williams was scandalized. She not merely understood what it meant perfectly, but she took the whole matter as coolly as though told her milliner had called about fitting on a dress. It was time he asserted his position and vindicated his respectability ; so he ventured,

"These things are very unpleasant, ma'am."

Dolly looked at him and understood that, shown the slightest loophole of an excuse, he would have given notice on the instant. Now this was precisely what she wished to avoid. That the servants must be dispersed and the house dismantled she knew, but she wanted Leonora back amongst her own people, and the body of the poor pretender, who had wrought such evil for himself and others, laid in its quiet grave before the work of destruction commenced, and so she answered,

" Yes, indeed, Williams, they are and must seem particularly unpleasant to you. I ought to have thought of that. I will see this person myself." And before Williams could interpose, or by look or hint explain to her how much worse than improper he considered her personal interference, she had descended the staircase and was crossing the hall.

At sight of her the man rose from his seat, and believing her to be Mrs. Werner, he began some awkward apology for his presence.

Then Dolly explained she was only a friend staying in the house; that she feared at so late an hour in the evening it would be useless sending for Lord Darsham, and that in short, she worded it delicately but explicitly, he had better do whatever was necessary, and go about his business.

Which without the slightest unnecessary delay he did. First he opened the outer door, and whistled for his man as if whistling for a dog. Then he made a rapid inventory of a few articles in the dining-room, and after handing a paper to Mrs. Mortomley, took his leave.

Then appeared Williams, more erect in his respectability, more severe in his deportment, more correct in his speech than ever. He had made up his mind. He would give notice to Lord Darsham in the morning.

"Where would it please you, ma'am, for that person to pass the night?" he inquired.

Dolly went out into the hall where sat one of the men who had been such unwelcome visitors at Homewood.

Recognising her, he stood up and touched his forehead respectfully.

"It is you then," she remarked; "that is fortunate. Of course, there is no necessity for you to remain here."

"I am afraid I must, ma'am, orders is orders, and—"

"You can leave quite easily," she interrupted, "and you know that. You can come back in the morning. You must dress in black and wear a white cravat, and ask for Mr. Williams, and the servants will imagine you come from the undertaker. I will give you a sovereign if you oblige me in this matter, and

I am sure Lord Darsham will not forget you either. Take the key with you if you like."

Still the man hesitated. He looked at the sovereign lying in his hand, and then at Mrs. Mortomley. Then he ventured,

" Is—is there anything else in ? I know you are a lady as wouldn't deceive me."

" Nothing," she answered.

" Or expected ? " he went on.

" There is nothing expected," was the reply. " But something may come, although I do not think it in the least degree probable. If it does, I will say you are already in possession; no harm shall come to you."

" I must stay for a little while, for fear of the governor coming back, but I will leave before ten o'clock if that will do ? "

" That will do," said Mrs. Mortomley.

What a contagion there is in vice !

As vice, or indeed as worse than vice, Williams regarded these mysteries with which Mrs. Mortomley was evidently *au courant*, and yet there seemed a fascination about it all to the butler.

As such things were to be, why should he
not master their details? Although he despised
the French, he knew a knowledge of their
language sometimes stood a man in good
stead, and in like manner if sovereigns were
being flung about in this reckless fashion, why
should he, through superior address, not have
the manipulation of them? His knowledge
of mankind taught him half-a-crown would
have compassed Mrs. Mortomley's desires as
completely as twenty shillings, and Williams
sighed over that balance of seventeen shillings
and sixpence, as Mr. Swanland had sighed
over John Jones' two pounds ten shillings.

"I want you, Williams," said Mrs. Mortomley, when his meditations had assumed the
form of regrets, and he followed her into the
dining-room.

"You had better let that man have some
supper," she said. "I suppose you can manage
to do so, and if for a day or two you are able
so to arrange matters that no one shall suspect
who or what he is, I am certain Lord Darsham
will be very much obliged. And I can only

say for my own part, I am very much obliged
and—" a slight pantomime of offer and protest
and final acceptance, and another of Dolly's
sovereigns had gone the way which so many
sovereigns, that can ill be spared, do go in this
prosaic world.

Williams did not give notice next morning
to Lord Darsham, and his forbearance was
rewarded.

CHAPTER XII.

MRS. MORTOMLEY BREAKS THE NEWS.

MRS. WERNER, clad in the deepest of mourning, in the most unbecoming of caps, sat in that small room where Dolly had overheard Mr. Werner's utterances concerning her husband. Her cousin had been closeted with her for nearly an hour. Faithfully he agreed with Mrs. Mortomley that he would break the news of the dead man's embarrassments to his widow, and, indeed, it was plain no time ought to be lost in acquainting Mrs. Werner with the actual state of her finances.

"She has ordered mourning for the whole household," observed Lord Darsham, "and she has intimated her wish that a milliner should go to Dassell to see the children's dresses are properly made. Now, with every wish—"

"I comprehend, my Lord, and have already countermanded her orders, or, at least, have requested that their execution may be delayed."

Something in the tone of her voice, something in the stress she laid on the words my lord, struck the person she addressed with a sense of uneasiness.

"Good Heavens! Mrs. Mortomley, you don't suppose I grudge Leonora this small expense. You do not think so meanly of me as that, I hope. But, still, with an execution in the house I cannot imagine that Leonora—"

"If Leonora knew how she is situated," Mrs. Mortomley again interrupted, "she would clothe herself in sackcloth; she would have all her coloured dresses dyed black rather than incur one penny of needless expense, and she ought to know, and you ought to tell her."

Which Lord Darsham finally agreed to do, and then left the revelation to Mrs. Mortomley.

"She must be told, and at once," thought Dolly, as she dragged wearily up the staircase, to find Mrs. Werner sitting in her widow's weeds, all alone.

"Lenny," she began, "I want to speak to you very seriously. I think you ought to go back to Dassell without any unnecessary delay."

Mrs. Werner half rose from her seat.

"Are any of the children ill," she asked, "or is it my mother?"

"Your mother is well as far as I know," answered Mrs. Mortomley, "and so are the children; but there are evils almost as hard to bear as illness, and—"

"You know, Dolly, I can bear anything better than suspense," said Mrs. Werner.

"I know nothing of the kind," was the was the reply. "My own impression is, you or any woman could endure suspense better than bad news, and my news is bad."

"What is it like?"

"It is very like a change of fortune," answered Mrs. Mortomley. Did it never occur to you, Lenny, that of late you have been living at a tremendous rate?"

"I was aware we spent a considerable sum of

money," said Mrs. Werner; "but Mr. Werner wished it; and his business was good, and—"

"My dear," interrupted Dolly, "his business, poor man, was not good. He was forced to keep up an appearance in order to preserve his credit, and he was far from being rich when he died."

"You are not in earnest?" asked Mrs. Werner, an expression of horror coming into her face, for which her friend knew too well how to account; then added, "Oh! Dolly, tell me the worst at once?"

"I do not know either the best or the worst myself yet," was the answer. "Only of one thing I am certain, that you and the children are not left so well off as we might have hoped would be the case."

"That was what Charley came to tell me a little while since," remarked Mrs. Werner.

"Yes, his heart failed him as mine would have done, Leonora, but I felt you ought to know."

"Dolly, do you think this had anything to do with his death?" asked Mrs. Werner, so suddenly that the question taking Dolly unprepared she stood mute, unable to answer.

"You *do* think so then?" said Mrs. Werner.

"I only think, remember, Leonora. God alone knows."

"Leave me," entreated the miserable woman. "I will try to bear it, but, oh! leave me to bear it alone."

Dolly crept down to the drawing-room, where Lord Darsham anxiously awaited her return.

"Have you told her?" he asked. "Has she decided on her future plans?"

"I have told her as much as I can tell her at present," was the reply. "When she has recovered a little from the shock, she will form her plans, no doubt. Meantime, my Lord, I think I could help you, and Leonora too, if you would tell me your plans with regard to your cousin and her family."

"Before I answer your question, will you answer one of mine? What have I done, Mrs. Mortomley, that your tone and manner have changed towards me so utterly? You are misjudging me in some way. You fancy be-

cause Leonora is poor, I shall not be so willing
to help her as if she had been left well-dowered.
Is it not so?"

"'Conscience makes cowards of us all,'" remarked Dolly, with a bitter little laugh. "It
is you who have changed. Poverty and money;
these two things are the touchstones of love,
esteem, friendship. Have I not seen it? Do
I not know it? I was wrong to expect a miracle; but I did hope for better things from you."

"And what have I done to forfeit your good
opinion?" he asked. "Could a brother have
taken more responsibility upon himself than I
have done? I would have paid out that fellow
downstairs, but you advised me not to part
with money which might be useful to Leonora.
Have not I told you I will see to her and the
children? Is it not merely to save her annoyance I urge the necessity for her departure
from this wretched house? Surely, you are
hard to please?"

"I am not at all hard to please, and you
know that," she answered. "When first you
heard of Mr. Werner's reverses, you were good-

ness itself; you were as utterly unworldly and disinterested as—well, as my own husband is.

"But you had not then stood face to face with that ruin which overtakes a commercial man. A loss of income; the reduction of a household; having to live frugally, and dress plainly; these things never seem terrible to friends and acquaintances who are not called upon to practise such economy in their own persons. What has tried you is just what tries every one who is privileged to see the process by which men, unable to meet their engagements, are stripped of everything they possess.

"That man in possession horrified you almost as much as he did Williams. Being brought into contact with Mr. Forde disgusted you. Lord Darsham began to wonder with how much of this sort of thing he might become connected, and, though quite willing to do his duty, he could not avoid thinking duty a very unpleasant necessity."

"You are exhaustive, Mrs. Mortomley."

"It is a subject I have studied," she said. "Do you suppose any human being could pass through all this, as I have done, and come out innocent and believing. The bulk of friends I class under two heads :—those who know, and those who do not know what ruin means. The first simply turn their backs on the ruined man altogether ; the second ask him to dinner, or to stay with them for a week, a fortnight, or a month."

" I am not going to ask my cousin to dinner, neither do I intend to turn my back on her," he remarked, unable, angry though he was, to avoid smiling at Dolly's sweeping assertions.

" No, but what are you about to do for her ; what are you able and willing to do for her ? If you mean—supposing she is utterly beggared —to say, I will allow you so much a year certain, say so to her soon. If, on the other hand, you are uncertain as to what you can do in the future, let her think if there be any way in which she can help herself, and assist her to the best of your ability. You would be doing her a greater kindness to leave her to let lodgings or keep a school, than to make her a pensioner on your—kindness shall we say ?—for an uncertain income."

Lord Darsham took a turn or two up and down the room, then he said,

"You hit hard, but you hit fair. I will consider what I ought to do, and can do; and then—"

"It will not cost you much," she observed as he paused. "A woman may care for these things," with a gesture she indicated the furniture and appointments of that stately room. "Most women, I suppose, do like pretty and costly surroundings, but if she be a woman like Leonora she can give them all up when she knows it is right she should. You cannot imagine how much we can do with a little when necessary. Do you recollect sending Leonora a hundred pounds last Christmas?"

"I do, and she gave it away, and I was angry with her in consequence."

"She gave it to me," said Dolly boldly, though her face flushed a little as she made the confession. "And do you know what I did with it? I started a business—a colour manufactory—and we are living on the profits of that factory now, and when my dear husband gets strong again, I shall be able to begin and pay that hundred pounds back to Leonora.''

"She won't take a penny of it," he exclaimed."

"Yes she will," answered Mrs. Mortomley, " because we understand each other, Leonora and I! Shall I ever forget that Christmas Eve! I had five sovereigns between us and nothing. A husband making nothing, and ill, and obliged to go up each day to see the trustee of his Estate. I was miserable. I was lonely. I was wishing I had been brought up to work of any kind, so that I might earn a few shillings a week, when Leonora came,— Leonora in her silks and furs, with her dear kind face ; and she would make me take your cheque, and I declare, when I opened and looked at it, after she drove away, I felt as if it and she had come straight from God."

" Dolly," he said, " had I only known—"

" You might have brought me more," she went on ; " but you could never have brought it in the same way. She knew all ; she had seen the bailiffs at Homewood; she had seen friend after friend desert us; she had seen insults heaped on our heads; she had seen her own husband turn against mine when misfortunes overtook us; but it made no difference with her, and for that reason I shall stand between Leonora and trouble so long as I am able."

It was inconsequent language; but Lord Darsham knew well enough what she meant by it. He had felt that if being mixed up with business and Mr. Werner's affairs, and Mrs. Werner's adversity, included executions for debt, and interviews with such men as Mr. Forde, and taking the sole charge of his cousin and her children for life, then indeed he had become involved in an affair much more disagreeable and of considerably greater magnitude than could prove pleasant, and he had felt compassion for himself at being placed in such a situation.

But Dolly, the Dolly he remembered when she was but a tiny bit of a child—in the days in which his cousin Leonora called her Sunbeam—had put the matter in its true light before him.

If he was going to do anything for his cousin, he ought to do it efficiently. Dolly, as he himself said, hit hard; but she did hit fairly. As she put it, he was free to do or he was free to leave undone; but he was not free to allow Leonora to feel his kindness a burden, her position insecure.

No, Dolly was right; the matter ought to be put on a proper footing. It would never do for him to pay this, that, and the other, and in his heart feel Mrs. Werner, whom he once wished to marry, was spending too much money. Even in that matter of dress, Dolly's common sense had stepped in to the rescue.

"Mrs. Mortomley," he said at length, "will you go with Leonora to Dassell, and when I have arranged affairs here so far as they are capable of arrangement, I can follow you and we shall be able together to decide on our future plans?"

"I should not like to go," Dolly answered; "but if she and you wish it I will go."

As it proved, however, nothing on earth was further from Leonora's desires.

"I cannot return to Dassell yet," she said to her friend. "Mamma's questions would kill me. Dolly, will you take me home with you, to-morrow?"

"Aye, that I will, darling," answered the brave little woman, utterly regardless of ways and means in her anxiety to pleasure that distracted heart.

"Stay with me for a little while, please," whispered Mrs. Werner. She was afraid, now she had once looked upon the face of her trouble, of being left to contemplate it through the darksome hours of the summer night.

"I am going to sleep on the sofa, and if you want me at any hour or minute you have but to say 'Dolly.'"

Next morning a curious discovery was made. Mrs. Werner's jewellery, which she never took with her to Dassell, had all disappeared.

This led to an investigation of the contents of the plate closet, which seemed extremely short of silver, but this Williams explained by stating that when the family went to Brighton the previous winter, his master had for greater security removed the bulk of the plate to his bankers.

These matters were not mentioned to Mrs. Werner, but they filled Lord Darsham with a terrible uneasiness.

He felt thankful that his cousin was leaving that huge town house which lawyers and auctioneers, and bankruptcy messengers, were soon to fill with their pervading presence.

"May I come and see you, Mrs. Mortomley?" he asked, as he bade her good-bye at the Great Eastern terminus.

"Certainly," she answered. "Our cottage is a small one, but, as the Americans say, it opens into all out of doors."

He retained her hand for a moment, looked earnestly in her face as she said this, then the train was off, and, she smiling at him, bowed and kissed her finger in acknowledgment of his uplifted hat.

They were gone, and he walked slowly out of the station full of a fancy her words had conjured up.

CHAPTER XIII.

SAD CONFIDENCES.

WINTER was gone, spring had come, and if the song of the turtle dove was not heard in the land, the wood-pigeons made noise enough about the Mortomleys' house to almost deafen its occupants.

Spring had come, spring in its garments of vivid green, decked and studded with primrose stars; spring, bringing the perfume of up-springing sap, of tender violets, of early hyacinths to refresh the sense; spring with its promise of daisies and buttercups, of fragrant hawthorn, of budding wild roses.

With everything beautiful decking the earth in honour of her advent, spring came smiling that year across the fair English landscape. Sunshine and blue sky everywhere overhead; underfoot springing grass and luxuriant wheat and flowers, and bud and leaf; and at the first, and when the first spring bird's twitter announced that the loveliest season of all the English year was close at hand, Dolly's spirits rose like the heart of a giant refreshed to give the sweet visitor greeting.

She had been ailing and languid all through the tedious winter, but at sight of the sunshine, at sound of the songs of birds, somewhat of her former brightness returned.

"I know now," she said, "how glad that poor dove must have been to get out of the ark. I never used to be tired of winter, but latterly the winters have seemed so long and cold and dreary."

"And yet we have kept up glorious fires this winter," remarked Mortomley, to whom health and comparative youth seemed to have been restored as by a miracle.

"Yes," agreed his wife, "what should we have done without the great logs of wood—

and you—aunt?" and she held out a grateful
hand to Miss Gerace, who never intended to
go back to Dassell any more, who had given
up her house, her maid, her furniture to 'the
ladies,' as they were styled in that far-away
region, Mesdames Trebasson and Werner; who
never intended to leave Dolly again, and who
had with tears in her eyes entreated her niece's
forgiveness because she had, thinking Mrs.
Mortomley could never come to want, sunk
the principal of her money in an annuity.

"You dear old thing," said Dolly trying to
laugh away her own tears, "when you are lost
to me and mine, we shall not cry the less because you could not leave us enough to buy
mourning," and it was then Miss Gerace
and Dolly agreed they were not to part company again.

In good truth, how Dolly would have got
through that winter without her aunt's presence and her aunt's money she did not know.

Life had been a hard enough struggle
when she was strong to battle, but not long
after Mrs. Werner left the little cottage, Dolly

felt a weakness come upon her against which she was impotent to struggle, which made it easy to persuade her to take her morning cup of tea in bed, and do little save sit near the grateful warmth of that pleasant wood-fire through the day.

The doctor came ; a pleasant chatty country doctor, who was accustomed to patients who liked to dwell on their ailments, and who, though Mrs. Mortomley puzzled him, never imagined she could be so stupid as to tell him fibs.

According to all known rules Dolly ought to have had one or two very sufficient pains, one or two very decided symptoms, but Dolly had no pains and no symptoms. She was only tired she declared, exhausted mentally and bodily if he preferred that form of expression, and she should be well in the spring.

That was all any one could make out of Mrs. Mortomley, and when the spring came it seemed to justify her prediction.

With the bright weather Dolly revived. She sat in the sunshine, she donned her brightest apparel, she ate with a relish the simple country fare, and she requested the kindly rector to say one day from the reading-desk that Dollabella Mortomley desired to return thanks for "mercies vouchsafed."

"For what mercies, my dear?" asked the good rector, who could not look at her wistful, eager face quite unmoved.

"God has vouchsafed me another spring," she answered; "one of almost unalloyed happiness?"

And so the sunshine of old returned and stayed with her to the end.

With the spring came Mrs. Werner. Her friend had requested her visit long before; but she delayed complying with that request till an almost imperative message brought her South.

Then Dolly gave her that packet, the secret of which she had kept so faithfully, and when Mrs. Werner opened it, she found notes to the amount of two thousand pounds and a letter, her dead husband's confession and farewell.

"I cannot retain this money," said Mrs. Werner.

"Do so for a week and then we will talk about it," Mrs. Mortomley answered, and for a week the widow maintained silence, walking alone through those Hertfordshire woods, and for the first time keeping her vigil with the dead.

"Do not send that money to lawyer, trustee, or creditor, Lenny," said Mrs. Mortomley when they came to talk the matter over. "Remember your marriage vows and obey your husband. He risked much to save that for you; do not frustrate his intentions. When the expenses come out of that, it would be a penny in the pound to the creditors; and if you could send it direct to the creditors, they would not thank you for it. Poor Lang—oh how sorry I am Archie and Lang could not get on together, for he was one in a thousand—said to me once,

"'Look here, ma'am, creditors are this sort of folks. If you had paid them nineteen and elevenpence in the pound, and stripped your-

T 2

self of everything to pay them that, and they saw your clean shirt lying on the bed ready for you to put on, they would want the shirt on the bed to pay the odd penny.' Keep that two thousand pounds, my dear. I, who have been through it all, tell you any human being who allows sentiment to influence business pays for his folly with his life ?"

"Dolly !"

"I mean what I say, Lenny ; but you need not employ a crier to circulate the news. It will not be yet ; but it must be some time. Had we laid aside two thousand pounds, I might have lived to be as old as your friend the Countess of Desmond."

To Mrs. Werner the way in which those who were with Dolly continually, refused to believe in anything very serious being the matter with her, seemed at first incredible, but after a time she too found the fact of danger hard to realise. Death and Dolly appeared as far removed from each other as light and darkness, and yet she was going, surely, if slowly out of the day into the night.

" I am thankful to see her so much better,"
remarked Miss Gerace, in answer to some
observation of Mrs. Werner's. " She did look
shockingly ill through the winter. I was quite
uneasy about her, but now she has recovered
her spirits and her appetite, and is getting
quite a colour in her cheeks."

Mrs. Werner remained silent for a moment,
then with an effort she said, " Dear Miss
Gerace, can not you see what that colour is—
don't you know Dolly paints ? "

If she had declared Dolly to be a pickpocket,
Miss Gerace could not have been more shocked.
Forthwith she took her niece to task about
this iniquity, which Mrs. Mortomley did not
deny, though she tried to laugh off the accu-
sation.

" What is the harm of sometimes painting
the lily ? " she observed. " If Leonora had
either been as stupid or as wise as she ought
to have been, I should eventually have worked
up that colour to one of robust health, but as
you all appear to object to my looking beautiful, I think I shall take out my frizettes, let

down my hair, wear a dressing-wrapper all day long, and adopt the appearance and manners of an untidy ghost."

"My dear, you should not talk in that light way," expostulated Miss Gerace; "though you may not know it, illness is a very serious thing."

Not know it! There was a little quiver about Dolly's mouth which might have told a tale to the woman who had lived so long, if her understanding of her niece's nature had been as thorough as that possessed by Mrs. Werner.

Not know it! Had she lain awake through the long, long winter nights, and the scarcely less dreary spring mornings, reconciling herself to the idea of that long, lonely journey, thinking thoughts that lay between herself and her God, without coming to a full comprehension of the fact that not even sorrow is more solemn and awful than mortal sickness.

She knew all about it.

"But I never could bear the sight of sad faces," she said to Mrs. Werner, "and if you

frighten aunt and make Archie think there is
something very much amiss with me, you will
render all our lives miserable."

Mrs. Werner sighed. It was against her
preconceived ideas that a woman should smile
and laugh and be still the very sunshine of
her home all the time a fatal disease was
working its will upon her, and yet she felt in
her heart Dolly's was the soundest philosophy,
if only she could be induced to take care of
herself to lengthen out the time before ——

No, she could not even mentally finish the
sentence. If Dolly would not make an effort
to save her own life, some one should fight
against death in her behalf.

" It is wrong of you," she said, " knowing
how precious you are to us all; you should use
every effort to get well again. You ought to
have first-rate advice. You ought to have
change of air. You ought to have everything
nourishing and tempting in the way of food.
I shall take charge of you myself now. You
belong to me as much as to your husband. I
am sure no man ever loved a woman more
than I have loved you."

"Come here, Lenny," was the answer.
"Come close beside me, dear—here in the
sunshine, and let us settle all this at once,
never to speak of it again. For myself, for my
own very individual self's sake," she went on,
taking Mrs. Werner's hand in hers, and strok-
ing it absently, "I am not certain that if I
could, I should care to live, unless, indeed, I
were able to find some waters of Lethe in
which I might plunge and forget all the
misery, all the humiliation of the past. There
are some people who cannot forget. I am one
of them. There are some who cannot remember and be quite happy; that is my case.
There are some who think life not much worth
having unless they can be very happy in it; I
fear I hold some such heretical doctrine."

She stopped and kissed Mrs. Werner, smiling
all the time the bright smile of old.

"So much for myself," she said, "but for
Archie's sake, for Lenore's, for yours, not
least for the sake of my poor aunt who has
grown so to love me, just when it would have
been well for her to have done nothing of the

kind, I would stay if I could—I would spend money and time and thought, to get strong again.

" I have consulted doctors, I have told great physicians every symptom of my complaint, though I do not choose to be quite frank with a medical man, who, knowing Archie, might make the poor fellow wretched before there is any necessity for him to be told the truth.

" I have followed every scrap of advice so far as I possibly could, I have taken care of myself, and the result is I am here still ; and it may be, if affairs continue to go well with us, that I may remain for a long time yet, as time counts in such cases. And now, Lenny, do not let us speak of this ever again."

"But cannot you get away from this place?" asked Mrs. Werner.

" I am as well here as I should be anywhere else," was the reply; "and it would be folly to move to a fresh neighbourhood just when the works are really beginning to return a good income. Besides, though the house is small, I love it; and those woods are, to my mind, the very realization of peace."

" How did it happen Lang left you ? "

" I can scarcely tell you, such a variety of reasons went to make up the sum total of his discontent. Of course, till Archie took the reins, he had everything almost his own way; he bought and he sold and he kept the books and he employed whom he liked, and finally he lost his head as all people of his class do. I dare say you never had a cook able to grill a chop, who did not fancy you never could get on without her. Well, of course, Archie found this unpleasant. Lang got discontented and jealous and very troublesome, and made things uncomfortable for himself and every one else.

" At last matters came to a crisis about a clerk who had such good testimonials, we thought he would prove a treasure. We shortly found he was anything rather than a treasure however, and Archie would have got rid of him at once if Lang had not come up one evening and given us the choice of parting with him or Roberts—that was the clerk's name.

"He said, he Lang, need not remain long out of a situation; that Hart, Mayfield, and Company had offered him a good salary, and that if he was not put on some different footing with us, he would go to those able to appreciate his services.

"So Archie answered he had better go to them, and he went and we were all very sorry, Lang included,—he repented, and would have stayed at the last, but I don't see how Archie could have kept him."

"Neither do I," said Mrs. Werner; and then she asked "Now that Mr. Mortomley is making money, is he not afraid of Mr. Swanland demanding a share of the profits?"

Dolly laughed. "Everything is in the name of Miss Gerace, and you cannot think how pleased the old darling is when we joke about her colour-works and ask how orders are coming in for her new blue and her famous yellow. She is learning to write a plain commercial hand so as to take the whole of the correspondence. I cannot tell you the comfort she is to me. I do not know what Archie and

I and the child would have done without her all through the dull, dark winter days."

Mrs. Werner did not answer; she was wondering at that moment how Archie and Miss Gerace and the child would do without Dolly through the days of the sorrowful summers and winters yet to come.

CHAPTER XIV.

WHAT RUPERT HAD DONE.

MRS. WERNER had returned to Dassell carrying with her that legacy, the disposal of which was still as great a perplexity and trouble as ever. The hawthorn-trees were in full bloom, the dog-roses showing for blossom, the woods resonant with the songs of birds, and Dolly sat one day out in the sweet sunshine all alone.

She had wandered slowly through the woods to a spot where, the trees ceasing to impede the view, she could see far away over the luxuriant champaign through which the Lea wound its devious way, glittering in the distance like a thread of silver.

There she sat down to rest on a felled tree, and the beauty of the landscape stole into her heart, and with it a feeling of infinite peace. For the moment life and its cares, past troubles, the fear of sorrow coming to those dear to her in the future, dropped from off her spirit; as for a few minutes a heavy burden, that must be taken up again, may be cast aside. She felt better than she had done for months previously, and at once her buoyant nature grasped at the hope that perhaps her disease was stayed, that she might live a few years longer to see her husband again free, without that shadow of bankruptcy and unpaid debt pursuing him.

His discharge was the one earthly good Dolly still desired with an exceeding longing; and under that bright clear sky, with that sweet peaceful country stretching out before her eyes, even so wild a dream as freedom for the man she loved and pitied with a love and pity exceeding that of a wife seemed not incapable of fulfilment.

Along the path which, cutting first across

the fields and then through the wood, led straight as a crow's flight from the nearest railway station to the high-road, which their little cottage overlooked, she saw a man advancing towards the spot she occupied.

Not a young man, not a labouring man, not any person resident in the neighbourhood, but a stranger, evidently, for he often paused and looked around, as if doubtful of being in the right way, and when he had got a little distance into the wood he stopped and hesitated, and then retracing his steps, took off his hat, and asked Dolly if she could kindly direct him to

" Mortomley's Colour Works ?"

She gave him the information, and then added,

" If you want to see Mr. Mortomley, he is not at home to-day."

" That is very unfortunate," remarked the stranger.

" Is your business with him very important ?" she asked, a fear born of the experiences of that time she could never recall without a shudder prompting the question. "I am Mrs. Mortomley," she explained with a nervous laugh and a vivid blush. "Perhaps you could tell me what it is you want; and that might save you trouble and spare him."

He did not quite understand what she meant by her last expression. How could he tell that now, as in that far away time when Mortomley had been ruined, her first thought, her sole desire was to spare him, the man over whom a sorrow impended, the coming of which she could not retard?

"You are very kind," said the gentleman courteously; "but I could not think of troubling you about the matter. I must see Mr. Mortomley, however, and if you name a time when he is likely to be at home, I will call."

She felt certain, now, that something dreadful was about to happen.

"I wish," she said, rising; "I do wish you would give me some idea of the nature of your business. I am not very strong, and

I cannot bear anxiety as I used to be able to
do ; and if you will not tell me why you want
to see my husband, I shall be imagining all
sorts of evil. I beg your pardon for speaking
so vehemently," she added, seeing a look of
amazement in the stranger's face ; "but you
do not know what we have gone through."

Looking at her more closely he could form
some idea.

"Pray sit down," he entreated. "I am so
sorry to have alarmed you. Why you are
trembling as if you thought I meant to do
your husband some great injury, and I only
want to speak to him about a colour I understand he manufactures !"

"What—his new blue?" asked Dolly,
brightening up in a moment.

"No ; his new yellow," was the reply.

It would have been impossible for any one
to avoid being amused at the sudden change
in Mrs. Mortomley's expression, and almost in
spite of himself the stranger smiled as he
answered.

Dolly's face reflected that smile, and as he

saw the sunshine in her eyes uplifted to his,
the stranger, though he had come on no
friendly errand to Mortomley, felt himself
drawn by an irresistible attraction, to be
friends with Mortomley's wife.

"Won't you be seated?" she asked.   If he
had been young and handsome as he was old
and plain, Dolly would, without thought of
evil, have issued a precisely similar invitation,
and the stranger smiled again as he availed
himself of it.   And seeing that, Dolly smiled
once more while she asked him what he wanted
to say to her husband about the new yellow.

"I wanted to know, in the first instance, if
he really manufactured it," was the reply.

"Oh! yes; quantities," she answered.
"He could sell fifty times as much if he had
a larger place to make it in. Do you want
some?"

"No," said the stranger; "I do not."

Now this puzzled Mrs. Mortomley, and so
she tried back.

"What did you want to know in the second
instance?" she asked.

" Really, Mrs. Mortomley," he was beginning, when she interrupted him.

" It is of no use your trying to deceive me ;
you have got something unpleasant to say to
my husband—what is it ? "

" Well, the fact is, he has no right to be
making that yellow."

" He has every right," she retorted, " for
he invented it; and if you come from Mr.
Swanland, you can tell him that I say Mr.
Mortomley will manufacture any colour he
pleases."

It was a privilege accorded to few people,
but the new-comer certainly had the benefit of
seeing Dolly in all the moods of which her
nature was capable in a single interview.

" I do not come from Mr. Swanland," was
the reply; " indeed, I do not know who Mr.
Swanland is. That is my name," and he
handed her his card; " and the reason why I
say Mr. Mortomley has no right to make that
yellow is because he sold his secret to me."

Dolly looked at the speaker as a tigress
might have done had he touched her cub.

She got first red with passion, and then that red turned to a white heat, and her heart seemed to stand still with rage, then suddenly it gave a great bound of relief, and she said to that elderly gentleman quite solemnly, and yet with a certain cheerful assurance in her tone,—

"You are mad!"

"Indeed I am not," was the reply. "I hold a receipt for the money I paid for your husband's secret, and I think I have just cause for complaint when I find the formulæ given to me imperfect, and Mr. Mortomley sending a colour into the market which according to equity is mine exclusively."

"Show me the receipt you speak of," she said. "There is some great mistake—you are labouring under some gross delusion."

For answer he opened his pocket-book and handed her a paper, which proved to be a receipt for two hundred and fifty pounds paid by Charles Douglas, Esquire, for the formulæ of a new yellow.

This document was signed

"For Archibald Mortomley,
               "R. HALLING."

and in a moment Dolly understood what had been done.

"The viper!" she said; "and he knew we were beggars when he robbed us of the money. And we had sheltered him and his sister and—"

"For mercy's sake calm yourself, Mrs. Mortomley," entreated Mr. Douglas, as she broke into a perfect agony of grief. "I would not for all the value of the money, I would not even for the worth of the colour, have so distressed you. I will destroy the receipt and never mention the affair again if you will only promise not to fret yourself about the matter."

"You will not destroy that receipt," she said, rising. "You shall come home with me and hear how my husband has been cheated, just as you have been cheated."

In utter silence they walked together through the wood to the little cottage which was Mortomley's home, at sight of which Mr. Douglas experienced an amazement impossible to describe.

On the threshold Mr. Mortomley, who had returned unexpectedly, met his wife and her companion.

"Dolly," he said, "where have you been? what is the matter?"

"This gentleman, Mr. Douglas, will tell you," she answered. "He wants to speak to you about the new yellow."

"Yes, I came to have a talk with you on that subject, and unfortunately I met with Mrs. Mortomley on my way here; unfortunately for her, I mean, for I am afraid I have, most unintentionally, caused her great distress. I dare say you know my name as a colour manufacturer, Mr. Mortomley. I have long known yours, and I am very happy to make your acquaintance."

And so saying he held out his hand, and thus this man—good, generous, and rich—this man so wealthy that he could at the time of Mortomley's greatest prosperity have bought up everything he owned in the world, and scarcely have missed the amount, came unexpectedly into the lives of Dolly and her husband.

He had meant to curse, and behold he remained to bless altogether.

From the moment his eyes fell on Mortomley, he "took to him," as the homely phrase expresses that fancy at first sight some men experience for each other, and some women too ; and when from Dolly, at a subsequent period, he heard the particulars of that story I have tried in these pages to tell, his heart sank when he contrasted all he might and would have done for husband and wife with all he might ever do now, when it was too late to do much for one of them, at all events.

Fain would Mortomley with his wide charity, which, as Dolly declared, amounted in some cases to weakness, have excused and softened Rupert's perfidy ; but Mr. Douglas said, and truly, that the offence was one which admitted of no gentle shading—which was beyond excuse, "though," he added with a

kindly smile at Mortomley's troubled face, " I
see, not beyond your powers of forgiveness."

" I think forgiveness of injuries an entire
mistake," said Dolly from the depths of her
arm-chair.

"If so it is a divine one," remarked Mr.
Douglas. And then Mrs. Mortomley understood their visitor, who by that time had become their guest,—for all this conversation
took place after dinner—and the sister, of
whom he had spoken more than once, were
what she called, and often herself wished to
be, " good."

Nevertheless, she said subsequently to her
husband, " I shall tell Rupert what I think of
his conduct the very first time I see him.
You may forgive if you like, but I will re-
prove ; it only encourages people to be wicked
to be tender with their faults, and I do not
mean to be tender with him."

But when the time came she was not very
hard ; she said to him as they stood at the
gate of the cottage together, the last time he
ever saw her alive, " Rupert, I want you to

know we are not ignorant of how, when we were so poor, you sold Archie's secret to Mr. Douglas. Now, there are some things I can understand; I can under pressure imagine Lazarus robbing Dives, and a man in extremity forging and telling falsehoods to save his credit, but I cannot understand the nature of the person who shall steal twopence-halfpenny from the pocket of a blind old widow, or who, when the man who befriended him is sick and incompetent, takes that opportunity to rob him of the only possession left. You need not try to defend yourself, Rupert, because your conduct is indefensible."

"I shall not try," he said huskily; "I was wrong."

"That is enough; do not vex yourself about the matter now," she answered, "for, Rupert, unintentionally when you took Archie's ewe lamb, you gave him that which will turn eventually into a great flock of sheep."

CHAPTER XV.

MR. ASHERILL IS PERSUADED.

THERE could be no doubt but that Mortomley and Mr. Douglas were two men who ought, according to human wisdom, to have met earlier. Though a colour manufacturer, the latter had, through want of the inventive or combinative quality, been compelled to run in old grooves, while the former lacked precisely that firmness of character and mastery of detail which had made the northern merchant's fortune.

Mr. Douglas was one of those men who feel they cannot stand still and let the world get in advance of them, even though their pockets do chance to be stuffed with gold, and almost at the first glance, certainly after half an hour's conversation, he knew Mortomley was that other business half which himself required and for which he had been·vainly seeking through years among all sorts and conditions of men.

As has been said in an early chapter of this story, Mortomley's genius was essentially imaginative.

" Give him a laboratory and ease of mind, and there is scarcely a difficulty in our trade he could not overcome," thought Mr. Douglas. " If he can make a purely vegetable green, as he says he can, and I believe he says only what is literally true, he ought to make his fortune, and I should feel very much inclined to help him to do it." But when, subsequently, he broached this idea, Mortomley shook his head.

"I can never make a fortune unless I am able to procure my discharge, and if I live to be as old as Methuselah I shall never obtain that."

It was on this occasion that he gave Mr. Douglas a slight sketch of his experiences of

liquidation.   All the deeper tints, all the
darker shadows, all the lurid colouring, Dolly
added at a later period in the garden at Homewood, a place, Mr. Douglas said, he particularly wished to see.

Unknown to Mortomley, his wife and his
new friend travelled from a little country
station, then newly set up among the green
Hertfordshire fields, to Stratford, which Mrs.
Mortomley described in a brief sentence as the
"dirtiest place on earth," then they changed
carriages for Leytonstone, whence they drove
along the road Dolly remembered so well to
Homewood.

The hinges of the front gate were broken, and
they entered the grounds without let or hin-
drance.   Everything had been permitted to go
to wreck; the red-thorn-trees had been cut
down for fuel, the rare shrubs were hacked
and hewn to pieces, the great evergreens were
torn about or dead, the clematis and the
honeysuckle trailed along the ground over
part of the verandah, which had been dragged
down by the boys climbing over it; the laurel

walk was almost completely destroyed, and
upon the lawn, where beds filled with flowers
made the summer ever beautiful, a stray horse
grazed peacefully.

Within, the same tale of ruin was to be read
as they had found written outside. The
children who squinted and the mother that
bore them still were in residence, and there
was not a paper on the walls, not an inch of
paint, upon which defacing fingers had omitted
to leave a mark.

The kitchen-garden was a mass of weeds
and the drive knee deep in grass. Where
those children ought to have walked, they had
refrained from treading, but through the
shrubberies they had made a path, marking
their route, Indian fashion, on the trees.

In the remembered summer-house, where so
many a pleasant group had in the old times
collected, Dolly sat down to await the return
of their new friend.

He wanted to look at the "works" now
bare of plant, at the great yards once filled
with casks and carboys, alive with the stir of

workmen and the clamour of trade,—all silent
now, silent as the grave. At the time of
Mortomley's commercial death came the sleek
undertaker from Salisbury House, and took
away all they could bury of the man and his
surroundings.

Empty were the stalls of Homewood, bare
of oats the mangers, falling to decay the
pigeon-houses, tenantless the byres and styes,
denuded the barns, but in fancy Mr. Douglas
filled them all again with plenty and to spare.
Yes, he would buy the lease of Homewood,
and once again it should blossom as the rose.

He opened his project cautiously to Mrs.
Mortomley. The prospect of returning to the
beloved home might, he thought, prove too
much for her if the idea were broached without due preparation, so he tried, sitting in the
summer-house to lead up to it, but found his
auditor unsympathetic.

"She had loved Homewood dearly."

"Did she not love it now?"

"Yes, as one loves the dead."

"Should not she like to live there once
more?"

"No; she could never forget, never while life lasted, what she had suffered there."

And then she told her tale—told it looking with dry eyes over the desolate wilderness which had once been so fair a home—told it all, simply and without colouring, as a Frenchman might—supposing a Frenchman capable of telling an unvarnished narrative—relate how the Uhlans entered his modest habitation, and, not without insult, stripped it bare.

"But do not you think your husband would like to come back here?" he inquired after a long pause.

"Back here?" she repeated "I think I understand now your intention; but do not try to carry it out; Archie would never be happy here without me."

"Is your objection to Homewood, then, so rooted?" he inquired, with a disappointed smile.

For answer she only turned away her head, and he repeated his question.

Then she said, "I should not like my poor husband to arrange his future with any reference to me."

She had been so bright, so cheerful, so eager about Mortomley's prosperity, so reticent concerning her own ailments, that Mr. Douglas had learned to think he must have erred in imagining that when first he looked in her face he looked in the face of a woman for whom the fiat had gone forth, but now, by her forced silence, by the unshed tears in her voice when she finally answered, he understood.

He knew that she had faced her danger, and that to the last she was keeping a bold front to the enemy, for the sake of another; aye! ever and always, Dolly was faithful to that trust.

Without another word of explanation they left Homewood.

Tenderly, as she passed one special spot, Dolly gathered a sprig of myrtle, and kissing it, would have placed it in her purse, but, thinking twice about the matter, she held it in her hand till they were near the front gate, when she cast it from her.

Strong to the last, brave as tender, was it any marvel this man who had never called any woman wife, never held a child of his own to his heart, felt that had Mrs. Mortomley been his wife or his daughter, he could sooner have parted with life than with her.

"There is only one thing you can do for me," she observed as she lay back in the railway carriage on their way home. "Get my husband's discharge and that will be worth more than gold and silver to me."

"I will do my best, my dear," he answered; "but I fear the difficulties are almost insurmountable."

In truth he had been interesting himself greatly about this very matter, and he did not see, unless a useless expense were incurred, how the desire of Dolly's heart was to be compassed.

That fatal clause rendering the concurrence of the whole of the committee necessary had been paraded ostentatiously before his face by Mr. Swanland.

True, Mr. Kleinwort was not in England or likely to return to it, and Mr. Forde had nothing now to do with the General Chemical

Company, Limited, which had indeed itself ceased to exist, having been purchased by Hewitt and Date for a sum which paid the original shareholders about a sovereign in the twenty-five pound share.

The directors had made a gallant fight in order to continue the business, but their courage proved useless. The next morning after that night when Lord Darsham told Williams to show Mr. Forde the door, the manager had risen with the firm intention of handing in his resignation that forenoon, but on the way to St. Vedast Wharf he met Mr. Gibbons.

"Bad business that about Werner," said that gentleman.

"It's a bad business for me," answered Mr. Forde lugubriously; "I shall have to resign to-day, and what is to become of me and those poor creatures at home God alone knows."

"Nonsense!" retorted Mr. Gibbons; "why should you resign unless you have some consideration given you for doing so? Put a bold front on the matter, and say you did the best for the directors and the shareholders, and you are ready to answer any questions that may be put. They will give you a cool two hundred to walk out. That is what I should do if I were in your place."

And that was precisely what Mr. Forde did; the result being that he got not only two hundred but three hundred pounds given out of the directors' own pockets, if he would resign at once and follow his friend Kleinwort to South America.

And so that chapter in City history ended, with only this addendum, Mr. Forde never went to South America, though the directors said and believed he did.

With the three hundred pounds he travelled as far as Liverpool, where he set up in business with his correspondent Tom, and where people hear very little indeed about his wife and children, who live in an extremely small house situate at Everton.

Sic transit gloria mundi, the ex-manager might well exclaim, did he understand the meaning of that phrase, while pacing the pavement of those dreary streets to and from

his humble habitation, when he contrasts the
actual present with the once possible future
himself had conceived.

Mr. Forde's departure from London caused
another absentee; and as the opposition colour
maker had by this time gone into liquidation,
and would have cheerfully given his vote for
Mortomley's immediate discharge had any one
offered him five pounds, Mr. Swanland might
certainly have helped the bankrupt to freedom
had he chosen to do so. But Mr. Swanland did
not choose to do so, and Mr. Douglas was afraid
to tell Dolly this.

"It will come in time," she said calmly, " or
if it never does, some other way will open for
my husband."

"Yes," remarked her new friend, "I can
promise that, but you must promise in return
to go down to my little place in Devonshire,
and try to get well again. Smiles says, change
of air may do wonders for you."

Smiles was an eminent doctor, the kind old
man had feed liberally to come to Wood Cottage and pass his opinion upon Mrs. Mortom-

ley's state, and Mr. Smiles had said pleasant things, and deceived every one, save Dolly, as to her real condition.

Nevertheless, Dolly imagining the evil hour might be deferred, promised and fulfilled. She went into Devonshire, and with all her might tried to get well again.

The "little place" to which Mr. Douglas referred so carelessly, was as sweet a cottage ornée as eye ever rested on; and to say that Dolly revelled in the place and the peace and the scenery, is scarcely to convey an idea of the amount of happiness she contrived to extract for herself out of sea, and land, and sky.

There was but one cloud hovering over her, one worldly affair perplexing her, but that affair she meant to bequeath to Leonora Werner. Through Lord Darsham's influence and that of Mr. Douglas combined, she knew they would, with the facts she had jotted down, satisfy a second meeting of creditors that if Mortomley's estate in liquidation yielded nothing in the pound, no blame could be attached to Mortomley or Mortomley's wife; and that consequently,

according even to the wording of that iniqui-
tous Act of 1869, the bankrupt was entitled to
his discharge.

Between herself and her husband there lay
no secret. *She had told him.* One quiet Sunday evening she said simply, "It is best you
should know, dear." Her own hand dealt the
inevitable blow. It had to be given, and with
the subtle sympathy of old she comprehended
that if dealt by her, he would feel the keen
agony of the stroke less at the time, less in the
dreary hereafter.

"I shall stay as long as I can, Archie," she
added; that was all the hope she was able to
give him, and she gave it. She loved sitting
on the beach alone; that is, as regarded
her own friends and family, for she liked to
talk with children and grown-up people who,
unknowing of her danger and attracted merely
by her delicate appearance, made acquaintance
readily with the "sick lady."

Dolly liked to say she was better, and see
no sad wistful look follow her answer.

Amongst the few visitors to that remote

place was a lady with whom Mrs. Mortomley
delighted each day to exchange a few words.
She was old and prim, and fond of religious
conversation, and a trifle didactic; but Dolly
felt she was true, and Dolly had always liked
people who were genuine.

Perhaps that was the reason she was so
deeply affected when Lang came all the way
from London to see her and say " Good-bye."
He was to live in the Hertfordshire cottage
and work the colour manufactory for his own
benefit, and his old master had given him a few
specialities, and he would have been happy
but for Mrs. Mortomley's illness and the recollection of the gross perfidy of Harte and Mayfield, who had not merely sent one of their
own clerks to take service with Mortomley to
discover his secrets, but seduced him (Lang)
away with offers of higher wages, and then
turned him adrift the moment their purpose
was served.

"But, thank God!" said Lang fervently,
" they never could make the yellow—that
secret is dark enough still. I shall always

believe it was some blackguard from their
place frightened you that morning. I beg
pardon, you were not frightened, though any
other lady would have been."

And then they had much more talk, which
I have not space to repeat, even if I thought it
could prove interesting, and she sent the man
away with her photograph carefully placed in
a new pocket-book, in anticipation of becoming
his own employer

"Hang it up in some place for the children
to see," said Dolly; and it does hang up now,
duly framed and glazed, where not merely the
children, but all visitors can behold the like-
ness of Mortomley's faithful wife, which is a
digression from the elderly lady with white
sausage-like curls, who happened to be Mrs.
Asherill.

One day Dolly was sitting on the beach as
usual, when she beheld her nameless friend
walking towards her arm-in-arm with Mr.
Asherill.

Then Dolly, instinctively guessing the lady
with whom she had passed a few pleasant half

hours was the wife of that detested man, kept
her eyes so fastened on the book lying in her
lap that Mr. Asherill had a chance of passing by
in silence, of which chance he availed himself.

Not the next morning, which was Sunday,
but the next but one, Mrs. Asherill called at
the cottage and asked to see Mrs. Mortomley,
whom she found sitting in an easy-chair near
the window.

"I was not well enough to go to the beach
to-day," said Dolly, holding out her hand.
"How good of you to come here!"

"I could not rest without coming," was the
reply. "It seems dreadful that two people
like you and my husband should so misunderstand each other, as I am afraid is the case."

"Do we misunderstand each other?" asked
Mrs. Mortomley. "Sit down, Mrs. Asherill,
and imagine I am little Peterkin, and tell me
'what they killed each other for.'"

"I do not know exactly what you mean,
my dear," remarked the elder woman, "but I
have felt miserable ever since Saturday. My
husband spoke about you bitterly as I have

never heard him speak about any one before, and told me to walk in some other direction so that I might not have to speak to you again."

"And what did you tell him?" asked Dolly cheerfully.

"Oh! I made no reply. I meant to call and ask you when and why you had quarrelled, as I should so much like you and my dear, good, kind husband to be friends."

"Come," thought Dolly, "the man has one good point, he is kind to a woman neither young nor handsome; but perhaps she has money."

Which conjecture was true; but, on the other hand, he had been kind and tender to a woman without a sixpence—always ailing, always complaining, to whom he gave the best cup of tea—in those days of bitter griping poverty mentioned far, far back in this story.

"Till Saturday I did not know who you were," said Mrs. Mortomley, after a pause, "and I suppose you did not know who I was. In fact, neither of us was aware we ought to have waged war when we met, instead of sitting peacefully together talking on all sorts of topics. Now we have found out that you are you and that I am I. What are we to do? I am afraid we cannot remain good friends."

"But my husband could not avert your misfortunes. He told me distinctly he refused to undertake the management of Mr. Mortomley's affairs, and that it was quite against his wish Mr. Swanland meddled in the matter."

Dolly sighed wearily.

"I am afraid Mr. Asherill was right," she said, "and that you had better not have come here to-day. I do not wish to speak hardly of any man now, least of all hardly of any man to his wife, but still, I cannot help saying I think we have bitter cause to hate the very names of Asherill and Swanland."

"That I am sure you have not," answered Mrs. Asherill—"at least, not that of my husband. I must tell you something, just to show how utterly you have misjudged him. Do you remember a particularly wet Saturday in September, 18— ?"

"Perfectly," said Mrs. Mortomley. "I shall never forget it."

"Nor I, for that day I heard of the death of an old and very dear friend—about the last friend left—whom I had known since girlhood. That evening Mr. Asherill returned home much later than usual, and very much depressed. After dinner he explained to me that he was much concerned about Mr. Mortomley, whose affairs had fallen into embarrassment, and he proposed that we should send fifty pounds of poor Rosa's legacy as an anonymous present to his wife. Now, my dear, no doubt you never guessed from whom that little offering came?"

"I certainly never did, and for a sufficient reason," was the reply, "It never reached me."

"Ah! you forget," said Mrs. Asherill; "no doubt you had enough on your mind at that time to cause you to forget even more important matters than our poor gift—for it was mine as well as his; but I can recall the circumstance to your recollection; you will remember all about it, when I say you acknowledged the amount, with grateful thanks, in the 'Daily News.'"

"I never did," persisted Dolly; "such an occurrence could not have slipped my memory. I never received that money—never acknowledged having received it. I do recollect—" she was proceeding, when she stopped suddenly.

In a moment she understood the position, but she was not mean enough to take advantage of the opportunity thus presented. She could not tell Mrs. Asherill the true version of the affair; she could not ring the bell and bid Esther bring her dressing-case, and produce from the place where it had lain so long, John Jones's letter enclosing two pounds ten.

"There has been some great mistake about this matter, Mrs. Asherill," she said after a pause. "I never received that fifty pounds; and I should like to have an opportunity of speaking to Mr. Asherill on the subject. Ask him to call here next Saturday. Tell him I

shall take it as a great kindness if he will
favour me with a few minutes' conversation.
I have no doubt," added Dolly a little hypo-
critically, for she wanted to send poor Mrs.
Asherill away happy, "we shall be able to
arrive at some understanding." And she
stretched out her hand, which Mrs. Asherill
took and pressed ; then, moved by some im-
pulse she could scarcely have defined, she
stooped down and touched the lips of Mortomley's wife, murmuring,

"I wish—I wish, my dear, you were strong
and well again."

"Do not fret about me," was the quiet
reply. "I shall be well—quite well, some
day."

For the remainder of that week Dolly employed herself at intervals in writing. She
was always jotting down memoranda; always
asking Esther questions about what was done
and left undone after their departure. She
wrote to Lang, and received a perfect manuscript from him in reply. She wrote to Mr.
Leigh, asking him to search the 'Daily News'

of a particular week in a particular year for an advertisement which she specified, and by return of post that was forwarded. Finally, she sent a note to Mr. Asherill, directed to Salisbury House, and then she waited patiently for Saturday.

On the evening of that day Mr. Asherill presented himself at the cottage.

He came intending, spite of the character for sanctity he maintained, to tell many a falsehood in explanation of aught which might seem strange to Mrs. Mortomley; indeed, to put the case plainly, *any* falsehood which might best serve his turn.

His wife had, of course, communicated to him all Mr. Mortomley's wife had said to her, and he walked over to the cottage, thinking how, with his best manner, he might humbug the little woman Mr. Douglas had taken under his fatherly care.

But Dolly's greeting surprised him.

"Thank you very much for coming, Mr. Asherill," she said, holding out her hand; "I think we may shake hands now, for do you know, I fancy I am at the present moment a better Christian than yourself."

"It fills my soul with joy to hear you say so," he was beginning, when she interrupted him.

"I want to speak to you on business very important to myself," she said. "I want you to do something for me; I did something for you the other day—I kept silence when speech would have made your wife miserable. I did not show her John Jones' letter; I did not tell her of the first advertisement in the 'Daily News;' I did not even try to unmask you; so having established a claim on your gratitude, I want you to gratify the request of a dying woman, for I am dying," she added, speaking with the utmost calmness.

"God bless me!" exclaimed Mr. Asherill, surprised for once out of his worldly and religious conventionality.

"I do not think He will," said Dolly gravely, "unless you alter very much indeed."

"I was not thinking of myself when I made so unmeet an exclamation," he explained.

"Oh! of me?" remarked Dolly. "Yes, indeed, what I said was quite true—I shall not be here very long, and I am afraid I cannot go quite happily unless I see some near prospect of my husband obtaining his discharge."

Hearing this, Mr. Asherill shook his head—he was sorry—he feared—he lamented—but he felt compelled to say, he saw no chance of Mr. Mortomley ever getting free till he had paid ten shillings in the pound.

Then Dolly showed him her hand—showed him the memoranda she had made, the evidence of utter incompetence, of gross mismanagement, of senseless neglect that might be laid before another meeting of creditors.

She showed him that with energy and money the story of Mortomley's Estate might be made something more real than an empty tale; something out of which a man's freedom unjustly withheld could be justly purchased.

"You can get it for him without all that

Mortomley's Estate.

fuss and trouble," she said at last wearily, folding up the papers and laying them aside. "It is to be done quietly, I know; and if you like you can do it."

He remained silent for a few minutes, then he spoke—

"I do not like talking about business on a Sunday, but still this is a work of necessity. I will think the matter over and see you again to-morrow."

"Very well," answered Mrs. Mortomley, adding slily "this is a work of very great necessity."

Mr. Asherill thought it was, at all events. He did not like the turn affairs had taken; and the more he reflected, the more inclined he felt to throw Mr. Swanland over and take sides with Mortomley.

He had, after a fashion, hunted with the hounds, but now, he believed, it might prove both more pleasant and more profitable to run with the hare.

He retraced every step already trodden by his firm. He calculated every inch it would be necessary for him to travel in the future, and the result was, he said to Mrs. Mortomley,

" I think I can do what you require. Some money may be necessary, but perhaps I had better see Mr. Douglas about that ? "

" Yes," agreed Dolly, " or Lord Darsham, he has promised help if pecuniary help is needed."

CHAPTER XVI.

CONCLUSION.

It came one glorious morning towards the end of August, when the sunlight was dancing over the Lea, and there was a glory of brightness on the earth as well as on the water.

Mrs. Mortomley sat in an easy-chair drawn close up by the open window, and every now and then those around looked at her with furtive and apprehensive glances. There was no longer any effort at disguise. Her aunt, Mrs. Werner, Mr. and Miss Douglas, Mortomley himself, comprehended the end was very near, and only little Lenore was kept in ignorance. Dolly insisted upon this and on having her sent to Dassell till all should be over.

"God bless you, my child!" was the mother's farewell, uttered without a tear.

She wept her tears afterwards when she was all alone.

"I do not feel nearly so well this morning," said Mrs. Mortomley at last. "I do wish, oh! how I wish that London letter would come!"

"Never mind the letter, dear," entreated her husband.

"But I must mind," she answered. "I have so hoped it would come in time."

"So it will," said Mr. Douglas kindly, "you may be quite certain of that, my dear."

She murmured some words, the sense of which was only caught by Mrs. Werner.

"Not in my time, though."

At that moment the post arrived, and amongst the letters was that Dolly had hoped she might live to read.

Her husband was free, and with a happy smile Dolly leaned back in her chair and scanned the lines as well as weakness would let her.

"You ought not to have risen this morning," said Miss Gerace severely.

"Oh! aunt, I was so weary of the night," and then they looked at each other sadly.

"I wish you would all go away and leave me with Archie," said Mrs. Mortomley, after a short pause, and accordingly they went, and husband and wife were left alone.

She had nothing to say to him. If she had she could not have said it to him then. He sat holding her hand in his, and she lay, her head resting on the back of the chair, her figure supported by pillows, her eyes closed, hovering as if loth to go, on the very confines of that life which had to her been so full of joy, and so full of sorrow.

All at once she half raised herself from the chair, and, turning towards her husband, said,

"Archie," whilst her whole face seemed to beam with love and happiness.

She had never, when he was near, left Homewood without turning at the gate to smile and wave her hand to Mortomley; and it seemed to him then, and he will always retain the pleasant fancy, that from the very shore of Eternity, with the glad light of Heaven shining upon and beautifying her face, she spoke that one word, she turned back for an instant to smile farewell.

THE END.

PRINTED BY TAYLOR AND CO.,
LITTLE QUEEN STREET, LINCOLN'S INN FIELDS.